By JULIA LONDON

Lear Family Saga Series
Material Girl
Beauty Queen
Miss Fortune

Highlander Lockhart Series
Highlander Unbound
Highlander in Disguise
Highlander in Love

Over the Edge Series
All I Need is You
One More Night
Fall Into M

Desperate Debutantes Series
The Hazards of Hunting a Duke
The Perils of Pursuing a Prince
The Dangers of Deceiving a Viscount

The Cabot Sisters Series
The Trouble With Honor
The Devil Takes a Bride
The Scoundrel and the Debutante

Homecoming Ranch Series
Homecoming Ranch
Return to Homecoming Ranch
The Perfect Homecoming

Lake Haven Series
Suddenly in Love
Suddenly Dating
Suddenly Engaged

Highland Groom Series
Wild Wicked Scot
Sinful Scottish Laird
Hard-Hearted Highlander

Also Available

7 Brides for 7 Soldiers

JACK

7 Brides for 7 Soldiers, #5

JULIA LONDON

One

*M*arch

Jack Carter was looking forward to meeting up with one of his oldest friends, Ryder. As soon as he hit Eagle's Ridge, he was going to walk right into the No Man's Land diner and order a burger, just like they used to do when they were kids. And then, he pictured that he and Ryder hopefully would meet up with some of the guys, whoever was in town, up on the ridge. They'd drink a few beers, throw a log or two on the fire, and look down at Eagle's Ridge and where they'd grown up. They'd reminisce about school, and sports, and the first girls they'd ever touched, and their lives in the armed services after that.

After meeting his friends, his plan was to surprise his widowed mom, and crash in his old bedroom.

Just like he used to do.

Even after the fiasco of renting wheels, Jack felt confident. The car business had happened in Seattle. He'd been surprised at how many people wanted to get out of town early on a Saturday morning. The rental counter had been so crowded that Jack had somehow ended up in the back of the room, penned in by restless travelers, next to a plastic fern in a corner. But he'd managed to keep his cool, had managed to rent a car in spite of perspiring profusely. He'd thrown his bag into the backseat, and with a death grip on the wheel, he'd driven out of that crowded garage, down that crowded street, and out of a crowded town.

As soon as he'd cleared town, he'd texted Ryder, told him he was on his way.

Can't wait, man, Ryder had texted back.

It had been a few years, that was for sure. To say Jack was looking forward to this mini-reunion was an understatement. He missed his best buds—Ryder, the brothers Zane and Adam, Wyatt, Ford, and Noah. He'd find time to swing by and see Lainey, too, one of his first real girlfriends.

He missed Eagle's Ridge, missed being part of a community.

He missed being the guy he'd been before he'd joined the Marines.

It was a beautiful day, perfect for a Founders' Day celebration. Ryder's grandfather was one of the founders of Eagle's Ridge. It was hard to imagine the old guy was still alive, but then again, Jack remembered him as tough as nails. He'd been an Air Force pilot during World War II and used to tell them amazing stories. He probably had a few more now. Jack was looking forward to this—it was going to be fun.

But when Jack drove into town, he was surprised to see that traffic was crawling in both directions down Main Street. Founders' Day weekend had always been big in Eagle's Ridge, but Jack wasn't expecting anything like this. The event had grown—tents and pavilions had been set up on both sides of the river. Main Street, with its collection of trendy restaurants and eclectic shops, was limited to foot traffic, and even that was already pretty thick.

To get to No Man's Land, Jack would have to join that stream of humanity and walk up Main Street.

No big deal, Jack told himself. He could do it—it wasn't that far. He parked his car and got out, and joined the crowd. But as they moved along like one corporate body, Jack's skin began to feel itchy. He felt hemmed in again, and shoved his fisted hands into his pockets and tried to focus on his breathing. He was a head taller than most, so he could see pretty well. He could see Sentinel Bridge, which he'd have to cross to get to No Man's Land.

His pulse began to ratchet. *This is not a big deal. This is Eagle's Ridge, asshole. You're in the Blue Mountains, as far from enemy territory as a person can get, so calm the hell down—it's been two years, man.*

The internal chastisement worked for all of a minute. But then someone laid on a car horn, and all of Jack's rational thought shut down. His heart went haywire, speeding up, then skipping around, then failing to beat at all. He struggled to get air in his lungs and broke into a cold sweat. He was *not* going to lose his shit in the middle of Main Street, and yet, he couldn't seem to stop himself. His vision blurred to the point that he could hardly see in front of him. His legs felt numb. He had the single, horrifying thought that he was going to faint. *Jesus, Mary, and Joseph, he was going to pass out on Main Street, in Eagle's Ridge, on Founders' Day.*

Escape.

He turned around, knocking into a man so violently that the man stumbled and fell against the side of a building. The man shouted at him, flipped him off, but Jack didn't offer an apology—he was too desperate to get off that street.

"Move," Jack said through gritted teeth. "*Move, damn it.*" He was loping against the tide almost blindly, knocking against people in his haste. He was running before he realized he was. *Fight-or-flight, fight-or-flight.* He'd lost his fight—it had been consumed by fear somewhere along the way—and now all he had was flight.

When he reached the parking area, the line of cars trying to get in had grown even longer. He banged into his car and scanned the parking lot—there was one way in, one way out. *How would he get out?* He was trapped! Anyone with just a passing acquaintance with firearms could come in and start picking them off, one by one, and there wasn't a damn thing he could do about it.

He couldn't breathe. His heart was on fire. He clutched at his chest, certain he would die in a parking lot, gripped by a heart attack.

"Hey, buddy, are you okay?"

The voice was that of an older man, but Jack couldn't focus on him. "Heart attack," he croaked.

The rest of it was a blur. There were sirens, and then men around him, men in uniforms. If they were uniforms, he must be safe. *Was he safe?*

"Can you hear me?" one of the men asked.

Jack nodded. His head hit the wheel well of his car. He realized he was on the ground, gravel pressing into his body, and he had no idea how he'd gotten there.

"Are you taking anything?" the man asked.

Jack focused on him. *A paramedic.*

"Maybe some kind of beta-blocker?"

"What?" He was unable to form a coherent sentence.

"You're okay." The paramedic put his hand on Jack's shoulder. "It's okay."

It wasn't okay! Nothing was okay!

"We can take you in if you want, but your vitals are good. I'd check in with your doctor if I were you." The paramedic began to pack up his stuff. "You had a panic attack."

Jack's face flooded with heat. "No way." He didn't know what had happened, exactly. This wasn't the first time he'd had painful heart palpitations. But it wasn't a damn *panic attack.* That was impossible—he was not *that* guy.

Jack drove back to Seattle that night. He couldn't go near Main Street for fear of it happening again. He didn't try to see his mom, either, unwilling to discuss why he looked as if he'd just been beaten to death, to face the possibility that maybe he was more like her than he wanted to be.

When he finally reached home, he walked in through the door of his apartment, locked it, then slid down on his haunches and dry heaved. *What was happening to him*? He was an ex-Marine. He'd served two tours in Afghanistan. *How could this be him?*

It was then that Jack saw the text from Ryder.

Dude, where are you?

He turned off his phone and wearily put himself in bed.

Two

*S*eptember

When Whitney Baldwin received her list of Dinner Magic clients for the week, she rolled her eyes.

Not him again.

She didn't know what irritated her more—that this client could not be bothered to come out of his office to even say hello? Or how about, *thank-you for making my dinner*? Or even, *please, not so much curry sauce*? Because honestly, between Whitney and her cupcakes, that curry sauce was a bit much.

Or maybe it was the fact that his fat, floppy-eared dog, with the inventive name of Buster, insisted on sprawling in the middle of the kitchen so that Whitney had to step over him every time she turned around?

Or could it be the fact that he ordered the same three dishes every week: turkey sausage with peppers and onions, salmon over zucchini, and Thai red curry chicken?

Answer: all of the above.

When Whitney had taken this job at Dinner Magic a month ago, she'd understood exactly what it was: a meal kit delivery service that featured organic, fresh ingredients, easy instructions, and suggestions for wine pairings. Only this delivery service was a notch above the rest because it came with a cook. The website said they were chefs, but Whitney was no chef. Sure, she knew her way around a kitchen, and she could follow instructions as well as anyone. But she was a baker—she was the queen of pies and cakes and cupcakes. Not dinner.

Nevertheless, she'd be a "chef" until she found the right place to open up her bakery and coffee shop.

When she'd taken the Dinner Magic job, she'd believed it would be a cool job. She'd envisioned meeting interesting people who would introduce her to a social life in Seattle. She'd expected, like any reasonable person fresh off the boat from Orange County, California, that people who lived in flashy, shiny high-rise apartments with doormen would be flashy and shiny, too. Young and hip people with lots of money, brilliantly interesting careers, so many friends that they had to juggle them with a social calendar, and many exotic places to be. The kind of people who *needed* a doorman. The kind of people who would want a friend like her.

So far, she was zero for ten on that front.

First of all, the apartments in those shiny high-rises were uncomfortably small—much smaller than the average apartment in Orange County. And many of her clients were surprisingly *un*shiny. She counted among her regular clients a lonely old widower who liked sauerkraut with every meal and kept cans of the stuff stacked in his tiny pantry; a single mother with two of the brattiest kids Whitney had ever encountered (and if the little girl slapped her on the rump one more time, Whitney could not be held responsible for her actions); and a young lawyer who apparently only worked and worked out, judging by his apartment's distinctive gym smell and papers stacked everywhere. And who could forget the man who was convinced his lovely wife was having an affair and was determined that Whitney was going to help him figure it out?

But they all paled in comparison to *this* dude. Jack Carter was his name. Whitney had only seen glimpses of him, flashes of body parts, even though he was *in his apartment* every time she'd gone. The first time, Buster had been waiting for her in the open doorway. She'd stepped off the elevator, looked down the hall, and the dog had hauled himself to his feet and bayed at her. The moment she'd stepped inside the apartment, a deep, masculine voice that sounded as if it ought to be selling you a luxury car on TV shouted, "*I'm on the phone!*"

She'd craned her neck toward the voice, down a long hallway, and all she could make out was the bluish-white glow of a computer screen lighting a room. Everything else was dark. "Should I just...start?" she'd called out uncertainly.

At which point, a figure suddenly appeared in the open doorway, but it was so dark that she couldn't make out his face. She couldn't make out anything other than he was tall. And muscular. *Quite* muscular. Muscular like the men on the covers of romance novels and underwear ads. He wore cargo shorts and a white Henley with the sleeves pushed up to his elbows. It looked as if his hair brushed his shoulders, but she wasn't certain. He had one hand on the doorframe, as if he were holding himself there. "Just put it in the fridge," he said.

"The ingredients?"

"The meal." And with that, he'd disappeared back into the room.

"Okay," Whitney had muttered, and had turned toward the kitchen—and had tripped over the dog, banged her elbow on the edge of the bar and knocked over a stool. "*Ouch, ouch, ouch,*" she hissed.

"Watch out for Buster!" the man shouted at her from down the hall.

Whitney had glared down at Buster, with his droopy face and floppy ears, which only seemed to delight the canine. His tail swished with such alarming speed she thought he might take off and crash into the ceiling.

The next time, there was Buster in the open door, and a note on the counter. *Please put finished meal in fridge.* She'd looked down the hall and could only make out the eerie light generated by a computer screen. But she could hear the unmistakable *tap tap tap* of computer keys. No guy, just another shout to put it all in the fridge.

And that was the way it was every time she arrived at his apartment. She and Buster developed a relationship built around the bits of food she tossed in his direction while his owner stayed in that back room. It was all a little creepy, to be honest. Whitney imagined all sorts of things about Jack Carter: A physical deformity so grotesque that he couldn't show his face. A debilitating immune deficiency disorder so dire that the mere chance of contact with another human was lethal. A drug addict. An ex-Mafia guy in the Witness Protection Program.

After two weeks, Mr. Carter stopped leaving notes. Not a *hello*, or *put it in the fridge*, or *jump off a cliff.* She would call out that she was here; he would grunt or say something so monosyllabic that she stopped trying to figure it out. She cooked the meal, put it in the fridge, set out a pair of cupcakes like she did at every client's house, and left.

So great! Here was Mr. Creepy again on her client list. Whitney complained to the chef scheduler, or whatever they called the woman who told her where to go each week and emailed the grocery list. "I get him every week, and he's just weird," she'd said. "Plus, he orders the same damn thing every week."

"These hipsters and their clean diets. Look, e*veryone* wants the waterfront," the scheduler had said, as if there were hordes of people willing to prepare the Dinner Magic meals for the inadequate amount of money the chefs were paid. "You'll work your way up to that."

"I wasn't...that's not what I—"

"We'll be in touch next week," she'd said, and had hung up.

Whitney was *not* complaining about having the downtown area as her assigned territory. She was unreasonably thankful to have a job—*any* job. She would rather eat dirt every day for a year than throw in the towel and go home to Mom and Dad. So, she sucked it up like the buttercup she was, and summoned an Uber to take her to Whole Foods to buy some organic sausage.

It happened that Jack Carter lived in a building with a doorman close to the store. That was great, because it was Labor Day, and a march was blocking the streets. "*Equal pay for equal work*!" shouted a group of women walking past Whitney as she made her way down the street carrying two stuffed shopping bags, plus her tote bag. The tote bag refused to stay on her shoulder, however, and slid down her arm to her wrist and banged into her leg. Whitney gladly would have paid any of those women to help her carry the load.

By the time she reached Jack Carter's building, her auburn hair had blown across her eyes and was blocking her sight. Frank, the doorman, held the door open for her. "Hi, Whitney," he said as she banged through.

"Hi, Frank."

"Got your arms full, huh? Any cupcakes in that box?"

"I just happen to have an extra one." She winked. She put her load down, then pulled a small pastry box from the tote. From that, she withdrew a cupcake she'd fashioned to look like a hot air balloon.

"Awesome." Frank grinned. "Never seen anyone make cupcakes like these. Thank you!"

"My pleasure."

"Can I carry anything for you?"

"No thanks, I've got it." She put her tote bag on her shoulder and hoisted her bags.

Frank escorted her across the marble-tiled lobby to the bank of elevators and pushed the button. "I'll call up and let him know you're on the way," he said, as she stepped into the open elevator. He waved as the doors closed.

The ride up to the eighteenth floor was silent and smooth, and the doors slid open onto a carpeted hallway with access to four apartments. Whitney stepped out, adjusting the bags in her hands again. She really needed to get one of those rolling coolers, which, of course, someone had suggested to her on her first day on the job. But she was trying to hold on to every cent where she could—renting and renovating a bakery was going to be expensive.

She started down the hall and realized that Buster, who usually waited for her in the open doorway, was not there. And the door was closed.

She put everything down when she reached the door, shoved her hair out of her face, and knocked.

She waited, hands on hips. There was no answer, no panting dog. She glanced at her watch. She was not late, she was prompt—four o'clock, Monday afternoon, the time *he* had selected. He was supposed to be here—that was the rule. You miss your time, you miss your supper. Whitney knocked again and waited.

Nothing.

She tried the handle, more to confirm her suspicion he was gone than to actually open the door, but lo and behold, it swung open and banged against the wall with a thud, startling her. "Sorry!" she shouted into the apartment. "Hello? Mr. Carter?"

It was eerily quiet.

"*Great*," she muttered irritably. It was a strict rule that Dinner Magic cooks were not to enter empty houses or apartments. But she was meeting her friend Louisa—who happened to be her realtor—at six, and she didn't have time to wait around. Nor was she particularly inclined to come back later. And what was she supposed to do with all the ingredients she'd just bought?

Whitney debated the rules vs. convenience. Her misgivings aside, she was not going to let Creep Factor Four make her lose out on pay. So she squatted down, picked up the bags with an *oof,* and walked into his apartment.

Inside, she slid the bags onto the bar and deposited her tote bag onto a stool. She peered down the hallway, but there was no blue glow of a computer. She thought about walking down there to have a look, but that seemed a little too invasive.

Instead, she removed her jacket and began to take out the things she'd need for the meal. She put the cupcakes she'd made on a plate, and slid that onto the bar. But before she dipped down to grab a skillet from the cabinet, she paused to glance around his apartment. It was nice, especially compared to some others she'd been in. The kitchen was small, but modern, with gleaming appliances and granite countertops. It opened into a living area with a view of the city and a glimpse of the waterfront where, at dusk, lights twinkled along the shore. Built-in bookcases stuffed with books and a few photos framed the fireplace.

Whitney had never ventured past the kitchen. She was usually intent on getting in and out, but today, curiosity got the best of her. So she was a snoop—she'd own it—but she was going to have a peek.

She walked across plush carpeting to look at the photos. One was of seven boys obviously taken several years ago, judging by their clothes. They were in a classroom. One of the boys had a black eye, and on the other end, one had a split lip. One stood in the back—he looked like the one in charge. The other four were arranged in various forms of insouciance and laziness, but one of them was grinning as if he knew something the others didn't.

There was another photo of a couple, their cheeks pressed together in a selfie pose. And a third framed photo of an older couple, seated in a typical Olan Mills fashion, man in back, woman before him, their heads tilted at strange angles. Last but not least was a picture of Buster the basset hound on a plush rug somewhere with a giant bone decorated for Christmas at his feet.

Whitney moved on to the books. Jack Carter apparently liked fiction, mostly military thrillers. There were also some history tomes scattered on the shelves, two atlases, a couple of do-it-yourself books, a few biographies and memoirs. She would have to give the creep props for at least being a man who read.

She started back to the kitchen but at the end of the bar, she happened to glance down the hallway. What did he do in that room with the computer? To have a look was invasive and rude and irresponsible. She was good and ashamed to even *think* it…but she still wanted to look.

Whitney took a few tentative steps in that direction, but she inadvertently brushed against her tote bag with her arm and sent it flying off the stool and crashing, bottom up, onto the tiled floor. She shrieked a little with the surprise of it, then quickly bent down to scoop up the contents that were now rolling around the tiled floor. A comb she never used, her wallet, her phone, a makeup bag, a pedometer that she could never remember to clip on, a little Lego man one of the brats had thrown into her bag, and a wire whisk that had made it all the way into the hall.

She was shoving it all back into her tote bag when the front door suddenly opened and a panting dog raced toward her and slid into her, licking her face before she could even register that she had company.

"*Buster*! All right already!" she exclaimed and tried to paw him off, but had to grab him by the scruff of the neck. "*Okay*," she said again, and scratched his chest before finding her feet. She wished for a hair tie, pushed her hair out of her face—and noticed the bare legs of a man.

Fabulous—this was how she would finally make his acquaintance, snooping around his apartment. She glanced up.

Well, *this* was a nice surprise—her client was *cute*. He had skin the color of a mocha latte and a smile so sparkling she was momentarily dazzled. "*Hi*." She beamed at him with a little more enthusiasm than she probably ought to have shown. "We meet at last!" She stuck out her hand. "Whitney Baldwin, at your service." *At your service?*

"At my service?" he echoed, taking her hand.

"I mean, we haven't actually met," she corrected, and shook his hand—heartily—before she let go.

"Yeah." He swiped off his beanie cap to run his hand through his hair. "I haven't walked Buster in a week or so. I guess Jack's been walking him."

Whitney blinked. "You're not Jack?"

The man laughed. "I'm Rain," he said. "His dog walker."

And just like that, a flock of wedding doves fell back to earth. Wasn't that always the case? The cute guy was never the one you were cooking for. "I'm sorry. I...I thought you were Jack."

"He's not here?" He sounded surprised. "He'll be back soon. He never goes far." Rain smiled, leaned down to scratch Buster behind the ears, then walked past Whitney, into the kitchen, and picked up Buster's dog bowl. He filled it with water. "Are you the housekeeper?" he asked. "I thought it looked a little cleaner around here."

"Ah, no. I'm with Dinner Magic."

"Dinner what?"

"Magic. It's a meal delivery that comes with a cook."

He looked utterly confused by that, but shrugged. "Sweet." He put the dog bowl on the floor for Buster. When he stood, his gaze fell to the cupcakes. Cupcakes were her specialty. Dinner Magic didn't know it, but she left a pair at every client's house.

"Would you like one?" She picked up the plate, offering them to him.

"Are you kidding? Yeah." Rain selected one and held it up. "A balloon! Very cool." He nodded with appreciation. "Thanks! Okay, gotta jet. I've got a date with a pair of Dobermans. See you tomorrow, buddy," he said to the dog.

Buster responded with a thump of this tail. He'd already splayed himself in the middle of the kitchen, apparently spent from his walk.

"See you around, Magic," Rain said with a charming little wink, and passed her, leaving the scent of woods and sweat and man lingering in the kitchen.

"See you," she said dreamily, and watched Rain go. When the door closed behind him, she realized she was still clutching her tote bag, and shoved it onto a stool. "You might have mentioned your walker was hot," she scolded Buster.

The dog's tail thumped once on the floor.

"So what, you're going to just lay there and wait for scraps?"

"I think this is yours."

Whitney's heart skipped at the sound of a deeply masculine and oddly familiar voice. She whirled around, prepared to defend herself.

A tall man stood before her. His jaw was covered with the dark shadow of an afternoon beard, and he'd brushed his hair behind his ears. He wore a rumpled T-shirt and shorts. She knew the breathtaking man with the piercing dark-brown eyes and full lips was Jack Carter. She fleetingly acknowledged that he was *not* physically deformed, not even close. Neither did he look high—he looked as if he'd just woken up. But strangely, he was also sweaty, as though he'd jogged up the eighteen floors.

His appearance confused her. She glanced at the door Rain had just gone out. "Did you just come in? Is there another door?" She looked around her.

He didn't speak. He stared at her with intensity, as though he thought she was going to do something. He held something in his hand, and as he slowly lifted it and held out his palm, Whitney saw that he was holding a tampon.

She stared at the tampon. *Her* tampon, an escapee from her tote. And the realization left her momentarily speechless and unwilling to claim it. "That's not mine," she said.

One of his dark brows arched above the other. "It's definitely not mine." He leaned forward very carefully, his gaze still locked on hers, and put it on the bar.

He was staring at her so hard that Whitney self-consciously swept the back of her hand across her cheek, expecting to find something there, like another nose. "Why are you looking at me like that?" she asked.

The question seemed to surprise him. He abruptly straightened and shoved his hands in his pockets. "I…you…you're smaller than I thought, that's all."

"Smaller?"

"I thought you were bigger."

She glanced down at her average height, average body. "You thought I was *bigger*?"

He shrugged and pushed his hands deeper into his pockets. "You make a lot of noise."

"I do not make a lot of noise."

He gave a curt little nod as if to say she did.

"Okay, fine—I whistle when I work. But if I was being too loud, you could have come out and told me."

His jaw clenched. "I suppose."

He *supposed?* She opened her mouth to say something about that, but he said, "What happened to my cupcakes?"

Feeling a tiny bit miffed he'd judged her, practically sight unseen, to be big and loud, she flicked her gaze to the lone cupcake. "Technically, they're my cupcakes."

His brows dipped in confusion.

"And I gave one to your dog walker."

His eyes narrowed. "Is that allowed?"

"It's allowed."

His eyes narrowed more. "Is feeding my dog table scraps allowed, too?"

Whitney glared at Buster.

"He's allergic to chicken. It makes for a malodorous night," he added.

So Buster had betrayed her. "Sorry," she said. *Not sorry.* "I should get started." She turned around before he could make a federal case out of a few extra treats with that jarringly sexy body of his.

Three

Jack didn't know what the dinner girl meant by the cupcakes being "technically hers," but he did not want her giving them away. After he and Buster determined they were not poisoned, they were the food he looked forward to the most. First, they were delicious, perfectly moist, and always amusing. And second, those cupcakes were his damn beta-blockers, so it was a pretty big deal if one went missing.

"For the record," he said, "the cupcakes are the best part of this meal business."

Her face lit with unreasonable pleasure that he might prefer cupcakes to sausage. He had his issues, but he wasn't a moron. "*Really?*" she asked.

"Really," he said uncertainly.

She suddenly smiled with…what was that, *delight*? It *was* delight. He would have been suspicious of that, but she had a really pretty smile. And even if he hadn't been very suave about the tampon, her cheeks had taken on an appealingly rosy hue when she said it wasn't hers. He liked her long, shaggy brown hair, and her big gray-blue eyes that sparkled in the light of his kitchen. To think that all this time, he'd imagined someone more along the lines of a school cafeteria lunch lady. She was no lunch lady.

"*Thank* you! I make them myself. I mean, I actually bake them. From scratch. But not here." She waved off his oven. "At home. They're my thing. I'm Whitney Baldwin, by the way. And you have to be Jack Carter, or I'm having a very weird conversation with a stranger right now." She thrust her hand forward in greeting.

"Ah…" Jack wiped his damp palm on his T-shirt and reluctantly took her hand. "I'm Jack Carter," he agreed. He didn't say more, because he was suddenly very aware that her fingers were long and slender. He'd forgotten how soft and delicate a woman's hand felt in his. *Good God, was he holding on too long?* He *was* holding on too long, because she pulled her hand free.

"Well, it's nice to finally meet you." She smiled broadly at him. "Even if you did think I was big and loud. But to be fair, I thought something was wrong with you."

Was it so obvious?

"Not *wrong,*" she amended, and pushed her shaggy hair over her shoulder. "But maybe horribly disfigured?" She laughed, as if disfigurement was somehow amusing. "Because you never came out," she clarified, fluttering her fingers toward the hallway. "I mean, I didn't *really* think you were horribly disfigured—well, actually, I wondered once or twice—but I was just trying to guess why you didn't come out."

Her cheeks took on that rosy hue again, and Jack liked looking at her cheeks. And in truth, he was horribly disfigured—but on the inside. "Yeah." He ran his hand over the top of his head, uncertain how to explain himself. "I've, ah...I have some pretty hard deadlines for work." True. And yet, not so true. "That's why I've been getting a meal service. No time." So untrue. He shoved his hands in his pockets again, fisting them, gripping to hold on to himself. "You made the cupcakes?" he asked, focusing on the hot air balloon. "For me?"

"Well...not just you," she said with a bit of a giggle, as if that were preposterous. "For all my clients. I'm a baker. And a baker's gonna bake." She grinned. "Get it?"

Get what? What was he supposed to get?

"That's a play on a hater's gonna hate."

Jack stared at her.

"It's a saying." She made a strange little gesture with her slender hand. "A cultural reference."

What was she talking about?

"Oooh-kay," she muttered.

He wasn't following, but then again, Whitney was seriously attractive and that was interfering with his brain function. He hadn't been this close to a woman in a very long time. This woman was still talking about cupcakes. "Anyhoo, I make cupcakes because that's what I love. Baking. I'm a baker."

"A chef," he said, because that was what he'd been told by Dinner Magic, whose services he'd fully investigated. Whose service he'd finally chosen because the chefs were fully bonded and background checked, and their experience verified. He'd grilled the Dinner Magic offices on this particular issue.

"No, a *baker*. I'm not a chef at all," she said cheerfully, which only served to ratchet up Jack's anxiety.

He was very careful about what he ate. With Dinner Magic, he knew exactly what the ingredients were and that the chef knew how to prepare them so that he didn't get sick. He couldn't get sick, because if he did, he couldn't go to a crowded hospital. That was out of the question.

"Oh no…you wanted a *real* chef," she said, wincing apologetically. "I'm sorry. They *say* chef on the website, but seriously, any monkey could follow these recipes. *You* could follow these recipes." She paused, thought expediently about what she'd said, and blanched. She started to wave her hand as though she were trying to erase the words from the air between them. "I so did *not* mean that like it sounded," she said. "I'm not a monkey—you're *certainly* not a monkey. I was just trying to make a point—badly—that these recipes are delicious and easy to make, and you don't need a French-trained chef to make them."

He would be calling Dinner Magic first thing in the morning about this chef business.

"Okay, I'm going to stop talking now." She dragged her fingers over the crown of her head to pull her hair back. "Do you maybe have a crowbar I could use to pry my foot out of my mouth?"

Jack felt himself smile a little, which surprised him. Generally, at this point in a conversation, he felt so nervous he couldn't speak. "It's okay," he said. "I'm not offended at being lumped in with monkeys."

Did that sound strange? It sounded strange. Like he was often lumped in with monkeys.

Whitney cocked her head to one side, and he wondered whether she was putting it all together. *Doesn't cook, isn't disfigured, apparently never leaves his apartment, doesn't know how to shake hands anymore, is frequently lumped in with monkeys...*

"So! You're a baker," he blurted, fending off any conversation into his habits before any questions were asked.

"Yep!" She brightened again. "I'm actually working on opening my own bakery and coffee shop." She looked proud enough to bust a button or two off her blouse.

"Ah. The cupcakes," he said. It all made sense now.

"Not just cupcakes. Breads, pies, croissants, cakes—if you can bake it, I will make it."

Was that another cultural reference?

"Okay! Dinner," she said. "I'll get right on that." She dipped down to get a pan from his cabinet and stood. She suddenly laughed. "It's funny—all my clients like to talk. I mean *talk*. I don't invite it, I swear—they just start talking. Like, I have this one couple, and one day, she wasn't home, and he just offered up that he thinks she is having an affair!" She threw her arms wide. The pan she was holding narrowly missed colliding with his stainless-steel fridge. "What are you supposed to say to that, I ask you?" She stepped over Buster, who had assumed his position as kitchen floor mat. "Turns out, you don't have to say anything. I didn't say anything but 'oh wow' or something like that, and he just unleashed."

She put the pan on the stove and picked up a container of vegetables, then reached into his cabinet for olive oil, which she poured into the pan, and turned on the burner. "And then I have a client with these two awful kids—" She paused here to glance at him over her shoulder. "Not that there is anything wrong with that—don't get me wrong. I *love* kids. I hope to have a few someday." She turned back to her work and tossed the vegetables into the pan. "But those two? They will not leave me alone. They are punching or pulling on me the whole time I'm there, and talking, my God, those two little kids talk. And you know what Mom is doing while I slave away, making her family a casserole?"

Jack understood he was not supposed to answer. Maybe because Whitney didn't take a breath before she continued.

"She's pouring a giant glass of white wine, walking over to the couch, and planting her feet on the coffee table like those kids don't even exist. She treats me like a babysitter who brings food." She glanced back at him, her gaze flicking over him. "But I have to say, you've been the biggest mystery. I thought I'd probably never even meet you."

Jack's gut clenched. He forced a thin smile.

"You must have an important job." She began to sauté the vegetables. "What do you do?"

"Ah...I'm a writer."

"Writer!" She cast a look at him. "*That's* cool. Thrillers?"

"Thrillers?"

"You have a lot of them on your shelves."

He stared at her.

She suddenly blushed and made a serious study

of the contents of the pan. "I know, I shouldn't have looked at your bookshelves," she said quickly. "Sorry. It's just that I'm a big reader myself, and I was curious what sort of books you had. You've got a nice library here, by the way. So am I right? Thrillers?"

She was cute. More than cute. She was sexy in the tights and short skirt she wore. And she made killer cupcakes. But he hadn't counted on her being quite so...*chatty*. He eased onto a stool. "Articles, mostly—I'm a journalist."

"Oh! I had a friend once who—"

"Mind if I ask what's on the menu?" he interjected.

Her eyes widened. She stopped stirring. "You're kidding, right? It's Monday." She flashed a smile of amusement at him and Jack forgot what he'd asked. "You get the same thing every week! If it's Monday, it must be turkey sausage and vegetables in a creole sauce."

Her smile was like a light shining so brightly in his eyes that he had to look away. He glanced over the bar at Buster, whose ears pooled into brown puddles on either side of his head. "I just click on the pictures," he muttered.

"Well, the picture looks pretty good, I will admit." She picked up the recipe card and held it up, over the bar.

Jack didn't know whether he was supposed to take it or not. He hesitated, his stomach doing a little seesaw thing, as if this were a life-or-death decision. It seemed as if every day he discovered something else to be anxious about.

But the dinner girl put the recipe card down before he was forced to decide and turned back to the stove.

He was being weird, he knew. He was trying, but today had been an especially bad day. Jack had lost touch with his calendar. He hadn't remembered until after the dinner girl had banged into his house and sent him into paroxysms of fear that today was the day she came to cook.

Jack should have said something then, should have called out to her like he always did, but it had startled him so badly that he didn't speak. *Couldn't* speak. Instead, he'd ended up on the floor in the corner of the master bedroom, his legs crossed like a swami, his fingertips pressed hard together while he concentrated on his breathing. That's one of the things Dr. Pratt, his psychiatrist, advised him to do when he felt a panic attack coming on. Dr. Pratt had advised a lot of things, but so far, that was all Jack had managed to master. And for the record, it didn't help.

The thing was, Jack had been feeling pretty good. He'd had a long Skype session with Dr. Pratt on Friday. This morning, he'd actually gone out for a coffee and hadn't had any troubles. Yes, it was pre-dawn, five o'clock, and no, there was no one on the street. But he hadn't been out for a coffee in many days—okay, weeks—and he'd considered it a small victory. He'd walked right up to the counter of Coffee Corner, ordered the biggest Americano they had, and had walked right back out onto the street without so much as breaking a sweat.

It had been so easy that Jack had even toyed with the idea that maybe he was cured. Maybe the panic attacks and the fear of dying had all been a fluke. But then, Rain had come for Buster, because although Jack could still take his dog to the building's inner courtyard to do his business, he couldn't take him to the park across that street. Jack had met Rain at the VA hospital a year or so ago—a good guy, a vet like him. Rain was one of the lucky ones—he'd come back with a functioning brain.

Anyway, Jack had happened to look out his window after Rain and Buster had left and had seen the mob outside his apartment building, blocking traffic. A *mob.* An inexplicable, moving mob of people.

Jack's heart had begun to pound as though it were trying to break free of his chest and flee. He'd clutched at his chest, certain that this was the heart attack that would finally kill him, that this terror that gripped his throat in its jaws would suffocate him. In the midst of that, the dinner girl had come in, banging through the door and calling out a *yoo-hoo* or something like it. His thoughts had instantly gone to defense. *Protect, defend, protect, defend ...*

Thank God, he didn't have a gun. Thank God that some sane part of him—the part that was not the head case the rest of him had mysteriously become—knew that he shouldn't have a gun in his apartment, knew that this wasn't really an attack. It was just the girl who had come to cook his dinner.

Jack had heard the dinner girl moving around as he'd struggled to calm himself. And then he'd known another moment of sheer terror when he'd realized she was moving toward the hallway that led to the bedrooms. He could imagine nothing worse than being discovered huddling in the corner of his room, quivering like a fawn, his shirt drenched with sweat. Then came the crash of something being dropped and a lot of muttering, but his breathing was so shallow and quick that he couldn't exactly hear what was being said.

It wasn't until he heard Rain returned with Buster—his totally amateur, didn't-know-he-was-a-therapy-dog therapy dog. But that was beside the point. Somehow, Buster knew just what to do when Jack had one of his episodes. He knew to stick his snout under Jack's hand, to lick his leg, to press his body hard against Jack's until his breathing returned to normal.

Unfortunately, Buster had misguided priorities. As long as the dinner girl was here to cook up something delicious, he wasn't going to come and check on his master and help Jack get his bearings. As long as Jack hid every time she came, he wasn't going to know what was going on in his kitchen. Dr. Pratt had suggested that Jack ought to meet the dinner girl. She'd suggested that Jack would know what sort of threat she posed if he actually met her and looked her in the eyes. Jack said he was too busy, because Dr. Pratt didn't get what it was like living in Jack's head. Dr. Pratt had reminded Jack that he'd met lots of women and there had never been a threat.

That was true.

Dr. Pratt said he had to face his panic.

His brain had slowly returned to normal operations as he'd thought it through, and he could now truly believe that all that nattering in the kitchen meant things were proceeding as normal. He'd managed to get off the floor and walk into the bathroom to splash water on his face and pull a T-shirt over his head. He'd managed to walk out to meet the dinner girl and retrieve his dog. And now, here he was, sitting at the kitchen bar while she cooked his meal.

Stop staring at her ass.

He couldn't help it. Jack hadn't been around women in two years, which, granted, was a very long stretch for a guy who used to juggle one or two at a time. *"You're a lothario,"* Christie, his sister, once accused him after he'd dated her friend, Teri, and things had gotten hot and heavy between them.

"What's a lothario?"

"A guy with a zipper problem," she'd said, and had punched him in the arm.

"That's not very nice."

"I didn't say it to be nice," she'd said, and had huffed away.

Face your panic. Was he panicking? No, he wasn't panicking, he was just...worrying. He was worrying that he was making an ass of himself right now. He'd lost his panache. Dropped it in a parking lot, left it on a plane, shot it up in Afghanistan.

"A bakery," he blurted. It was neither a statement nor a question.

She glanced over her shoulder. "Yep," she said confidently.

"Where?"

"Well, I'm new to town, so I'm scoping things out. Do you have any suggestions for trendy neighborhoods?" she asked, circling a spatula in the air.

Jack felt flush under his shirt. He scratched his face, realized he hadn't shaved in a couple of days. "Umm...not really."

"No? That's okay. I'm meeting my realtor friend in a bit. She's got a couple of places near Pioneer Square to show me."

Jack hadn't been through Pioneer Square in a very long time. He hadn't had sex in a very long time, either. Although he didn't consider himself a pig, he couldn't stop looking at her perfect, heart-shaped derriere and thinking about just how long it had been.

"Good?" she asked.

He glanced up.

"Pioneer Square. I need a great location. I'm scared she's going to convince me to lease some place that won't work." She dropped the sausage in the pan, added a container of sauce and a package of seasoning. "And rent is *expensive.*"

He wondered why someone would move to a new city to open a bakery. Did Seattle have the highest pastry eaters per capita or something?

"These recipe cards say fifteen to twenty minutes to make this dish, but trust me, it is consistently more like forty-five." She covered the pan, then pulled a head of kale out of the box. Buster lifted his head, and as deftly as a professional baseball player, she tossed a bit of crumb of sausage to the dog without looking at him. As deftly as a professional baseball player, Buster caught it.

She chopped up the kale and stirred it into the mix. "Ohmigod, look at the time," she said suddenly. "That's what I get for talking instead of working, and I'm going to have to get through that street march."

"Street march?" Jack's heart leapt to attention.

"A march, a party, some Labor Day thing."

Jack blinked. It was *Labor Day?* When he lost touch with his calendar, he really lost touch. So, not a mob after all—Labor Day. Something inside him relaxed. "I…could finish up if you need to go," he offered.

She laughed, and stirred the mixture harder. "I can't let you do that! You're paying me to cook it, and *plate* it, and box up half and store it in your fridge, and then clean the kitchen. Why else would you pay thirty bucks for this? You could go down to the deli and get the same thing." She paused and considered the wall for a moment. "I guess I shouldn't say things like that."

Unfortunately, the corner deli was not an option for him. "Seriously, I can do it," he said. Actually, he'd prefer it. He didn't know how to slink back to his room while she was here and he didn't know how to stop looking at her body and imagining things that were doing him no favors.

"I appreciate the offer, but I'm pretty sure you won't plate it right." She smiled playfully.

That smile was like fat sizzling on a hot griddle, and he felt himself relax a little more. "Are you dissing my plate game? I can spoon sausage and vegetables into a bowl as well as anyone."

"See, that's where you're misjudging this." She pointed with her spatula. "You don't just *spoon* it. You have to *present* it. You would not believe the amount of training we get on presentation. And anyway, it's almost done."

She put a lid on the pan and turned back to the sink. She picked up a piece of bell pepper from the cutting board and tossed it high in the air. Buster's squat legs had to rev to lift him up and wheel him about in time to catch it.

"What do you think about downtown?" She leaned over to open the cabinet under the sink, which gave him a glimpse into her shirt and the very perky breasts there.

Breasts.

Damn it. It had been a very long time since he'd touched one.

She glanced up, caught him looking, and Jack's face flooded with warmth. He wanted to escape. *Could he leave the room now? Maybe the building? At least go down to the basement and wait by the trash dump until the coast was clear? How far would he have to go before he would stop thinking about having sex with her?*

"Downtown," she said.

Downtown! Was that sexual innuendo? His pulse quickened, other parts thickened.

"For my bakery?"

"Oh, ah…" He almost sighed with relief. "I don't really…I'm not into, ah…bakeries." And now he was speaking English as though it were his third language. *Fantastic.*

"Well." She smiled. "Maybe I can change your mind about that." She nudged the cupcake closer to him.

She turned back to the stove, turned off the heat, found a plate in his cabinet and slid half the dish onto a plate, nudging the sausage to one side. She placed the plate on the bar, took out the recyclable container and spooned the second half into it, taking a moment to arrange it. From her pocket, she whipped out a marker and jotted down the contents and date on the lid, then put the container in his fridge. In five minutes, she'd cleaned the kitchen and given Buster a good belly rub.

"Okay!" she said brightly, and popped up, gathered up her things and her tote bag. "It was really nice meeting you, Jack Carter. See you Wednesday?"

"Sure." He awkwardly stuck out his hand. The only problem was that her hands were full. So, he quickly raised his in a half salute with a nerdy flair, as if that's what he'd intended all along. "Thanks."

"My pleasure. Bye, Buster!" she said cheerily, and hurried out the door.

Jack looked at his plate. Then at Buster, who had moved around the bar to take up a position where Jack couldn't miss his woeful stare. "What just happened?" Jack asked.

Buster swished his tail.

What had just happened was that he'd had the first full-on chat with a woman besides his sister in more than two years. And for the first time in a very long time, he'd had some very robust thoughts about sex.

He wondered what Dr. Pratt would have to say about *that*.

Four

———◆———

Whitney liked to think that she was an enlightened person who could admit her mistakes, contrary to the advice of one of her law school professors, who had warned his budding attorneys against such behavior. "To admit error is to admit weakness," he'd said gravely.

Which was one of the many reasons Whitney didn't want to be a lawyer. First, it meant practicing law. *Ugh.* Second, people—generally lawyers in her experience, and her experience was vast, given half her family was lawyers—said bullshit like that all the time and actually believed it. Case in point: she'd mentioned that ridiculous piece of advice to her father during one of their many heated conversations about her unwillingness to take the bar and join the family law firm. "You would be wise to listen to your professors instead of your *gut*," he'd spat.

Oh, and third, cupcakes.

For the record, there was nothing wrong with her gut instincts, and her gut was telling her to take back every mean thought she'd ever had about Jack Carter.

She was ridiculous—she'd pictured some sort of monster hiding his hunched back and missing eye in the back room, and she could not have been more wrong. Jack Carter had turned out to be a bona fide hunk. A tall, muscular, well-built man, with dark-brown hair and coffee-brown eyes, a slight limp, and a sexy shadow of a beard.

There was, however, one *tiny-teeny* flaw in that hunk-a-hunk of burning love: He didn't talk. He just stared at her as though she were the one with the hunchback. Apparently, he was the kind of writer who sat hunched over a computer all day and didn't actually talk to people.

Unfortunately, his reticence to engage in conversation brought out her uneasiness. Whitney was the sort to talk when she was nervous. A lot. It was as if her tongue had a mind of its own, was determined to find a way to make her funny, delightful, and charming—even if it killed her and everyone else in the room. Why was it some people could charm at the drop of the hat, and people like her had to search around for it like a blind man searching for a door in an unfamiliar room?

Her Uber arrived three blocks down from where the march was happening. Whitney shoved her things into the backseat and climbed inside as her phone began to ring. "Have I missed surge pricing?" she asked the driver hopefully, digging into her tote to find the phone.

"Nope," he said. "Pioneer Square?"

"Pioneer Square," she confirmed, and fished her

phone out of her tote bag and looked at the display. She groaned, then reluctantly slid the phone open. "Hi, Mom."

"Hi, honey! Where are you?"

"In a car. I've only got a couple of minutes."

"It'll take twenty," the driver said.

Whitney glared at the back of his head. Okay, so she lied to her mother. But conversations with her mother had been excruciating lately.

"Where are you headed? To dinner with friends, I hope."

Her mother was obsessed lately with Whitney's lack of a girl gang. "Actually, I'm going to meet my realtor to look at a property, and then we're going for drinks."

"That's nice. Is it…never mind," her mother said.

"Why? What were you going to say?"

"Nothing. I don't want to upset you," her mother said soothingly.

"What, Mom?"

"I was going to ask if this property is more affordable than the last one. Your father says real estate is overpriced in Seattle. Honestly, sweetie, I don't know why you had to go *there*. You could have made your pies here."

She had to go *there* because her father was in Orange County. They weren't exactly on the same page, and Whitney had figured if she was ever going to make a go of "making pies," she needed to do it without him breathing down her neck. She'd chosen Seattle after researching the market for coffee shops and bakeries. Seattle was a thriving city with a strong millennial population, and millennials loved their coffee and sweets. "I didn't know Dad was so familiar with real estate prices in Seattle."

"See? You're upset."

"I'm *not...*" Whitney paused and drew a breath. She could imagine her mother standing in the kitchen, her slender body dressed in fashionable yoga-wear, one foot propped against an inner thigh in a tree pose.

"Your father and I just want what is best for you, Whitney. We want our children to excel in life and be happy."

"In a way you deem appropriate," Whitney wearily reminded her. They'd had this conversation a thousand times.

"In a way that is perhaps a little more substantial and rewarding than your cupcake fantasy, sweetie."

This was the thing that made her insane. To the Baldwins of Orange County, a desire to own a bakery was not a suitably lofty goal. That was something that lesser people did. *Baldwins* were lawyers, like her father and older sister, Taylor, or doctors, like her brother Cameron. "It's not a fantasy, Mom. I'm here. I have a business plan that you and Dad both agreed was a good one. I'm trying to excel and achieve and be happy in a way that *I* think is best for me."

"We are all very proud of you, Whitney."

She wished she had a knife she could plunge into the headrest in front of her. They were not proud of her. What they wanted was for Whitney to be a lawyer, to join Dad and Taylor in the family law firm. Or, she could be a heart doctor, like Cameron. Dad had been laying out her path all her life: for example, she had to take ballet lessons because elegant little girls become elegant socialites. She had to join the Young Republicans because the Baldwins were patrons of the Republican Party, whether that aligned with her beliefs or not.

She'd hated those things and more. She was not elegant like a ballerina—anyone who took a look at her generous butt and sturdy legs could see that. She was not the least bit political, and never had a clue what anyone was talking about when she had to attend those dinners with her parents. And still, Whitney had played along, because Taylor and Cameron had before her, and because she thought that's what she was supposed to do. She went to law school, and a month after her last exam, when she was studying for the bar, she realized just how much she hated law. *Hated* it. And if she didn't cut bait then and there, she'd be stuck practicing law for the rest of her life.

When she announced what she really wanted to do, the thing for which she had a true passion, her father said she'd be the laughingstock of the family. He warned her that he would not bankroll this ridiculous dream, and that without his considerable resources, she'd never make it.

He was right in a way—Whitney would never make it with his shadow looming over her. So, she'd done her research, packed up her life, taken her inheritance from her grandmother and headed for Seattle. So far, things weren't working out as she'd hoped, exactly, but she was out from under her parents' negativity and their lack of confidence in her.

"You know what, Mom?" Whitney said. "I'll call you later. I'm trying to juggle a few things here and really don't have time to talk."

"Whitney, don't hang up mad. I didn't mean anything—"

"Yep, I know," she said curtly. Of course her mother meant something—she always did. "It's just that I'm super busy."

"Well…okay. But please call when you have time. I miss talking to you!"

Whitney would enjoy talking to her mother much more when she had her bakery up and running. But for now, she said good-bye.

Yeah, things weren't going as exactly as she'd hoped. She made peanuts at the Dinner Magic job, couldn't sell her baked goods to coffee shops or grocery stores until she had a kitchen that the health department would okay, and the days were ticking by. She wasn't ready to throw in the towel just yet, but if something didn't break soon, she didn't know what she'd do.

She tossed her phone in her bag and looked out the window. Her mind drifted back to Jack Carter. She'd much rather think of him than her own boring issues. How was it that a handsome guy like that was tucked away in a room with a computer? How was it that a man who, by all rights, would have women fawning over him, could be so awkward? He was curious to her, a puzzle to be solved.

She was going to stop complaining to the scheduler about him, because she suddenly wanted to know what made a guy like him tick.

Five

In his bi-weekly Skype session, Dr. Pratt had asked Jack whether he thought he might develop a friendship with his chef.

"What's that supposed to mean?" Jack asked. "And she's not a chef. She's a baker." He thought about that a moment. "Maybe a cook. I don't know. But not a chef." He was a little fuzzy on the details because as she'd been talking, he'd been ogling her.

"I think you are familiar with the concept of friends?" Dr. Pratt asked. "Let me ask it another way," she'd continued with the patience of a grandmother. "Is she someone you'd like to talk to? Because this is a perfect opportunity to explore the anxieties you feel around others. Your apartment is a safe environment. You've determined the meal service is safe. The contact is for a short duration. When she comes back for salmon night, you might ask her what she likes to read."

Jack was mildly alarmed that Dr. Pratt knew Wednesday nights were when he had the salmon and zucchini dish. But never mind that—he hadn't been struggling with this weird anxiety for so long that he didn't know that *reading* was not how you started a conversation with an attractive woman. "Maybe." He shrugged, his gaze on his leg.

"Many women are readers," Dr. Pratt said. "It's not a silly question."

He remembered Whitney had said she was a big reader. He looked up from the study of his bare knee and eyed Dr. Pratt on his computer screen, thinking.

"Try it and see where the conversation leads you. The idea, of course, is to carry on a conversation without worrying about the interaction itself. And if you get to know her a little better, you will feel more comfortable."

Jack was beginning to despair that he would ever feel more comfortable about anything.

"You feel easy with Rain," she said.

How did Dr. Pratt always read him so well? "Well, yeah," he said. "But I *know* Rain. He's one of us."

"Maybe she's one of us, too," Dr. Pratt said.

No. Whitney Baldwin was not a soldier. He was fairly certain of that.

"Let's aim for a goal of two friends around whom you feel comfortable, okay?" She smiled.

Jack rolled his eyes. "I know what you're doing."

"What am I doing?"

"You're trying to make it sound like I'm not bat shit crazy."

"You're not crazy, Jack. You have an anxiety disorder. It's not uncommon, particularly after such a traumatic—"

"Yeah, okay, all right." He cut her off before she could say it. "I will ask her what she likes to read."

Dr. Pratt was silent for a moment. "Great," she said. "I look forward to hearing about it when next we speak."

Not great. I will have completely botched it by then.

He ended the session and sat back, thinking about what she'd said. How was this him? How had the guy once known as Romeo gone from living his life to slowly letting fear consume him? It had crept up on him—he didn't really know how it happened, or when exactly he'd shut the door on his life, because it had happened gradually. He didn't know how he'd come to accept that he needed help, either—real help, and not the online chat rooms with other vets he was lurking in, or herbal supplements he was taking. He'd been seeing Dr. Pratt since early summer at the behest of his sister, after he'd had a panic attack in a department store. He'd gotten turned around in the maze of displays and couldn't see the exit. He'd caused a scene; the police and store security had been called, and he'd been forced to acknowledge that this thing in him was growing like a beast and consuming him.

In some ways, his bi-weekly sessions with her were great, and made him look at situations differently than his brain wanted to. But sometimes he wondered whether Dr. Pratt was really helping, because look at him—he couldn't even talk to a woman.

That woman would be here at four o'clock today to sear his salmon and sauté his zucchini.

Jack thought about what Dr. Pratt had said. He thought about it all day, even practiced having a conversation in his bathroom mirror. "So…what kind of books do *you* like to read?" He sighed. "Dude—you sound like some creepy stalker in a library." He studied himself. "Hey, have you read *The Hunt for Red October*? No? *Jesus*," he muttered to himself. He sounded ridiculous.

Nevertheless, he showered and shaved, and put on a collared shirt, and pulled his hair back into a ponytail. He was not a trendy hipster, and he didn't generally wear his hair this long. But getting to a barber was impossible for someone with his *disorder*—God, how he hated the word—and he'd put off finding one who would come to his house and cut it for him. Like everything else, he worried who the person would be, what he'd say, and so forth. His head was a vicious, hard place to be.

At half past three, his phone rattled in his pocket. He was expecting a call from a source for an article he was writing about negligent care at a local veteran's health clinic. He dug the phone out of his pocket, but before he could answer, someone or something knocked on his door.

Jack's heart surged to his throat. It was too early for his dinner delivery. Frank wouldn't let anyone up without telling him. He quickly silenced the phone and put his back against his office wall. Sweat began to bead on his forehead as he tried to think logically.

The door clicked. Buster began to bark as the door swung open. Jack's heart pounded so hard now he thought he would faint. He looked wildly about for a weapon—he *always* looked around for a weapon he did not keep for fear of actually using—

"Jack! Where are—*dammit*, Buster, you almost made me fall!"

Jack released his breath. He stared at the ceiling a moment, willing his heart to a normal beat. He dug the phone out of his pocket and looked at the display. Yep, that was his source, all right. "Thanks a lot, Christie!" he shouted at his sister. He dragged his wrist across his damp forehead.

"What?" Her curly blonde head appeared in the doorway of his office, Buster beside her, wagging his tail and looking up at her with very soulful eyes.

"You startled me and I missed an important call."

She rolled her eyes and stepped inside. She wore jeans with holes in the knees, a snowy-white boyfriend shirt, and red Converse sneakers. "It smells like unwashed bodies in here, Jack. Can't you open a window or something?"

"No."

She walked over to his U-shaped desk, where he had two computer monitors—one for work, the other for gaming and video streaming. His desk was neat— the papers stacked in an inbox, the pens in a holder. He wasn't a freak about it, but if he kept everything in the same place, he didn't have to worry about losing it. Or that someone had moved it. Strange how these things had never occurred to him Before Afghanistan and now kept him up at night.

"Who would be calling? I thought you were down to contact with your shrink, your editor, and your dog walker."

He shot her a look. "I talk to the guys," he said defensively, referring to his childhood friends— Ryder, Noah, Wyatt, Zane, Adam, and Ford. Except that he hadn't talked to them but once, by phone, since he'd ditched Ryder on Founders' Day. And Noah, who called to tell him his cousin Lainey, who was one of Jack's first loves, was really sick. "And I really needed to take that call," he said.

"Call 'em back. I'm not stopping you."

He gave his sister a look that clearly conveyed he would drop-kick her across the room if she didn't cut it out. She returned his look with one challenging him to try.

Christie was the one person on earth who knew what he was dealing with. She lived way up at North Beach, and didn't come downtown often. Usually, she called him to harass him.

"Why are you here, again?" he asked.

"That is not a nice way to greet your sister," she said pertly, and sauntered across the room to him, rising up on her toes and kissing him on the cheek. "I was forced to come because you won't answer the phone half the time, and you haven't been to see your mother in weeks. You know she's afraid of driving and can't come here."

In Christie's book, their mother was allowed all the anxieties in the world. She'd had them all their lives. Anxieties he hadn't really noticed until he started experiencing them himself. But Christie didn't cut him the same slack—nope, he was an ex-Marine and should be able to muscle through. She was the one who'd found Dr. Pratt. She and her fiancé, Chet, were even paying Dr. Pratt, because Christie didn't trust him to keep up the sessions if she didn't. She knew her brother well.

"Do you have anything to eat?" She sashayed out of his room with Buster on her heels. Jack reluctantly followed her.

She went into the kitchen and opened the fridge door. "Looking pretty bare. Is your dinner girl coming?"

"Supposed to, yeah."

She withdrew a container and opened it, stuck her nose in it, then put it back. She closed the fridge and went to his pantry, and took out a bag of potato chips.

"Seriously, did you come barging in for a reason?"

"Yes. I wanted to see my brother." She sat down on one of the barstools with the bag of chips. "And I told Mom I'd check on you."

He sighed. It was hard to stay mad at Christie. She had a big, pretty smile that had always warmed him, even when she was a little brat following him and his buddies around. "Frank should have buzzed me to let me know you were here."

"It wasn't Frank. Some new guy." She paused. "Don't freak. He looks like he's twelve and he had on the uniform. He said he started Monday and Frank had stepped out for a moment. I convinced him to let me up." She smiled.

"He shouldn't have done that. This is a secure—"

"*Jack*," she said sternly. "You're in Seattle now, not Afghanistan. He's just a kid with a new job. He shouldn't have let me up, but he did. The world is still spinning."

"You mistake youth for innocence," he warned her.

"No, I don't. And I don't want to talk about your paranoia—"

"I'm not *paranoid*. I have a *disorder*—"

"Call it what you want, but I'm getting married in six months and I really, *really* need you to walk me down the aisle, Jack!" she suddenly shouted. "Mom worries about you all the time because that's what she does, and since you avoid her, she says it to *me*."

"Okay, all right." He held up a hand. "You're right." He took a seat next to her. "I know I'm a pain in the ass. But I'm working on it and I'm getting better."

She shoved the bag aside and swiveled around to face him. "*Are* you?"

"I went for coffee one morning. I had a conversation with the dinner girl."

Christie sighed.

"What?"

"Well…the coffee shop is literally downstairs. And the girl comes into your house, so it's not like you're actually getting out in the world."

He had not told Christie how anxious women— talking—made him now. "It's progress."

She gave him a dubious look. "But how are you going to walk me down the aisle if you can't go past the coffee shop downstairs? I really need this from you, Jack. It's important to me."

Jack's face heated with shame and the anxiety of just thinking about walking down an aisle. He didn't know how he'd face it, he didn't know if he could. Still, he managed a smile for his sister. "I don't know yet, but I will be there, Christie."

She leaned forward and looked him in the eyes. "Do you promise?"

The bile in his throat rose. "I promise."

She smiled sadly and pushed a bit of his hair from his face. "Chet and I love you, Jack."

He smiled dubiously.

"We do. We're proud of you and your service in

the Marines."

Jack waved her off and stood. There was nothing to be proud of—all he knew was that his time in the Marines had left him a mess. He was very lucky he was a writer and could work from home for a living, or else he'd probably be locked away in some hospital by now.

"Jack, I—"

The apartment call button interrupted her. He walked over to it and punched the button.

"Mr. Carter?"

"Hi, Frank."

"Sorry about your sister getting upstairs without notice. Tristan is new."

"Don't worry about it." He'd do enough worrying for all of them.

"Miss Baldwin is on her way up."

"Thanks, Frank."

Christie waggled her brows at him.

"Stop it," he said. "And behave yourself. It's only the dinner girl." Except it wasn't only the dinner girl. It was a woman he'd actually talked to. A woman with sparkling blue eyes and a body that made his mouth water, and who carried beta-blocker cupcakes with her. He suddenly wished Christie would go home.

But Christie said, "*Sure,*" and settled back with the bag of chips as if she were about to watch a show.

Six

The apartment door was open, as usual, and Buster sat at the threshold, his tail wagging so hard that by all laws of physics, he should have taken flight. "Hey, buddy, hey Buster." She dipped down to scratch his chest. "I've got something just for you." She reached into the pocket of her jacket and withdrew a bone-shaped biscuit. She'd taken a stab at dog treats yesterday, and although she couldn't be a true judge, Buster nearly took her hand off to get it, then quickly disappeared inside, his prize clenched between his jaws.

"I'm going to say that's a win," she said to herself, and stepped inside. "Hello!" she called.

Jack suddenly appeared in the hall before her. He looked... Well, he looked dead-on sexy. He was squeaky clean and had shaved and *man*, did those jeans fit him well. Come on, was she staring at his package? She wasn't staring—she was *drooling*.

"Ah…hi!" she blurted, and tried to pretend she was looking for something in her tote to hide her interest. "I wasn't expecting to see you."

"Bet not."

Wait a minute—Jack didn't say that. A woman said that from somewhere inside his apartment. A *woman*. Well, that was disappointing. Extremely disappointing. Not that Whitney intended to seduce her client, even if she'd had a couple of very expansive daydreams about this guy. So he wasn't as reclusive as she'd thought. She'd get over it—she was seventy-five percent certain she would. She plastered a smile on her face.

"Come in," Jack said.

Whitney hoisted her things and walked into the kitchen. Yep, there was a woman seated at the bar, stuffing potato chips into her mouth. She happened to be one of those women who could stuff with abandon and still look fantastic. She was also very cute, and Whitney had to hate her a little bit. No one should be *that* cute.

"*Hiiiii,*" the woman said with an enthusiasm that was hardly necessary.

"Hi," Whitney said. "Don't mind me. I'm just going to throw a meal together, then I'll leave you two alone." She put her things down on the counter.

"Oh, I'm leaving," the woman said through a mouth full of potato chips. "I guess Jack isn't going to introduce us, so I will. I'm his sister, Christie."

Sister! The heavens opened and pumped bright sunlight into Whitney's mood. "Oh! Nice to meet you," she said happily, then privately warned herself to turn it down a notch. "I'm Whitney. The cook." She removed her little cupcake box from the bag and placed it on the bar.

"Yep," Christie said. "I've heard about you."

Whitney glanced at Jack, who stood stiffly to one side, looking wound tighter than a clock, his hands shoved deep into his pockets. "I hope it's not my cooking." She laughed. Again, too happily. Too loudly. *Get a grip, Whit.*

"The cooking is fine," Jack said gruffly as Whitney opened the cupcake box.

Christie gasped so loudly that Whitney started. "What is *this?*" Christie cried, craning her neck to see the cupcakes.

"Cupcakes. I make them," Whitney said proudly. She pushed the box closer to Jack's sister. "They're a little added bonus from me to my clients."

Christie picked one up. Whitney had made a batch of yellow Minions from the popular kid movie, *Despicable Me.* "They are *adorable,*" Christie said.

"That one's chocolate. The other is vanilla."

"Jack!" Christie held one up to him. "I have to have one."

He looked at the cupcakes.

"You don't need two," she announced.

Jack slowly pulled his fists from his pockets and folded his arms tightly across his chest. He seemed annoyed with his sister. "Fine. Take it."

"What about Chet?"

"*Chet?*"

"It's so rude to go home with one cupcake." She took the other one, and cast a beaming smile at Whitney. "Chet is my fiancé."

Jack grunted. "I've already had to share my cupcakes once this week."

Christie took that as a yes, made a little squeal of

delight and put the cupcakes back in the little box. "Thanks! They're so cute, Whitney. You should, like, sell them."

"That's definitely the plan," Whitney assured her. "Enjoy!"

"In your house, not mine." Jack pointed to the door.

"Fine, okay, I'm leaving," Christie said cheerfully. She stuffed one last potato chip into her mouth and slid the bag across the bar. She swept up her box of cupcakes and gave her brother a playful shove as she walked past him. "Call Mom. Nice to meet you, Whitney!" she sang out as she walked down the hall. A moment later, the door shut behind her and Buster wandered back into the kitchen, melting on the tile floor with all four of his short legs spread out from his body like a rug.

Jack's cheeks filled with air, which he slowly released. He said sheepishly, "She's a lot."

"She's super cute. And she seems really nice."

"Yeah." His gaze did a quick flick over the length of her before he shoved his hands in his pockets and looked away.

Why was he so jumpy? She hadn't started talking yet, so that couldn't be it. "Ready for some salmon?" she asked cheerfully, mentally dry heaving at the prospect of yet another Wednesday night salmon dish.

"Sure."

Well, of course, because God forbid the man have any variety. She began to remove the ingredients from the grocery bag while Jack stood there, his gaze fixed on something in the living room. When he glanced at Whitney, he seemed startled that she was looking at him.

"Have you read *The Hunt for Red October?*" he asked.

A weird question, apropos of nothing. "Nope."

His shoulders sort of slumped and he shifted his gaze to his living room and the bookshelves there.

"But I saw the movie."

He jerked his gaze back to her, looking strangely surprised and grateful. How could someone as hot as this guy be so *weird?* Sexy and weird did not go together in her book, but it was so oddly intriguing. "It's one of my favorite movies," she added. That was a bit of a lie. She liked it okay.

"Mine too."

She thought he would say more—like why he brought it up, or what he liked about it, anything—but he didn't. "I'm more of a rom-com girl," she said airily. "Do you like romantic comedies?"

"Ah...yeah." He nodded slowly.

That was when words that surprised her tumbled out of Whitney's mouth. She couldn't begin to guess where they'd come from, but they presented themselves all the same. "Maybe we could see a movie some time."

There was a moment of highly charged silence, during which Jack gaped at her as though she'd just suggested they rob a bank.

Whitney's face quickly began to flame. "Or not," she quickly amended. "I'm new to town and I'm trying to make friends. Not that I think you and I are friends, because *obviously,* you're my client, and I'm your cook, and we are *not* friends." She laughed long and loud at the absurdity of that. And here she went, her mouth a mile beyond her brain. "But, you know, I was just thinking how much I like rom-coms, and then a thought occurred to me, and *boom,* out it came."

He still stared at her.

"I'm sorry if I freaked you out. Don't pay any attention to me. I do stuff like that all the time."

"You didn't freak me out," he said evenly. "I just…I wasn't expecting that—"

"Of course not!" she jumped in, just so he'd know that *she* knew how inappropriate that was. "People don't hire cooks and expect to get asked out on a…" Jesus, she almost said date.

"I'm not freaked out," he reiterated. But he looked as though he were. He couldn't possibly shove his hands in his pockets any deeper.

"No worries," she said, although she hated that phrase, because no one should judge another person's worry meter. Anyway, she was the one who should be worrying. First, she'd thought this guy was either physically deformed or a drug addict, and then was wildly attracted to him. Second, he could scarcely look at her, and still, she was asking him out.

Maybe something was wrong with *her.*

Whitney took the ingredients and turned around, pretending to begin meal preparation and wishing her face would stop flaming.

"The thing is, I have this really pressing deadline," he said.

Oh God, was he going to start an apology tour for turning her down? She had to nip this in the bud before she melted into a puddle of mortification and drowned Buster where he lay. "Deadline! What's your deadline?" She turned around and smiled. "What's it for?"

His gaze was on her mouth. "It's a special report for *Military Times,*" he said. "That's an independent news organization that covers all aspects of the military. I write for them. I'm doing an article about some problems with a veteran's mental health services clinic."

The room at the end of the hall was beginning to make more sense. "Interesting!" she said. He was still looking at her mouth, and she felt the warmth in her face slide down her spine. "You hear about it all the time, soldiers coming back traumatized—"

"It's salmon tonight, right?" he suddenly interjected.

A socially awkward writer. Somehow, that made sense to her. Weren't they supposed to be mercurial and a little off anyway? Wasn't that the way creativity worked? But still, this felt a little different than creativity at work. She stopped what she was doing and looked at Jack Carter. "Are you okay?"

He physically reacted to her question. His body recoiled, almost as if she'd shoved him. "What? *Me*? Yeah, I'm okay. Sure, I'm okay." He raked his fingers through his hair. "Why?"

"I don't know…you seem kind of nervous."

"*Nervous*," he repeated, and drew a deep breath. Buster suddenly hopped up and trotted around the kitchen island. Jack dipped down to pet him. When he finally stood, he did not put his hands in his pockets. He walked to the bar and braced his hands against it. He stared at her, as if he were trying to say something. And at last, he said, "I have a confession. I'm not good at small talk."

That was it! She should have guessed that. She smiled. "Well, me either, obviously."

He looked confused. "You talk a lot," he said carefully.

Whitney laughed. "Yeah, but I talk a lot about nothing. I have this awful habit of filling up silence, and it doesn't matter with what. My dad tells me all the time, 'not everything needs to be talked about, Whitney,'" she said, mimicking her father's voice.

Jack didn't have a response. He just studied her face.

"Like now." She gestured between them. "There's a *lot* of silence happening here."

"Some people could use a little more talking and a little less silence," he said.

Was he talking about himself? And was it natural for a man to have pillowy lips like that? "Allow me to do the talking then," she said. "I will start by telling you that I took the liberty of bringing a caper sauce."

"Okay," he agreed.

"I had this very salmon dish one night, and I had a caper sauce that I bought at Pike's Place because the guy told me it would transform any meat into a work of art, and do you know, he was *right?* And I thought, I know a guy who eats the same thing every Monday and Tuesday, every Wednesday and Thursday, and every Friday and Saturday. And I thought maybe this guy would like a little variety."

"He doesn't," Jack said.

She gaped at him. "How can you not want variety?" She began to chop the zucchini. "Will you just try it? I swear to you, it was fantastic."

"Why do you care if I have variety?"

"*Why?* Because it's weird that you eat the same thing week after week. It's a true lack of diversity, and no one wants to be the guy who lacks that."

His gaze seemed to deepen, locking on her eyes, and Whitney felt that sliver of heat in her spine begin to boil.

"I can safely say that no one has ever cared about my lack of diversity before."

"You need someone to care. Will you try it?"

His gaze moved to her hair, then to her ear. "What if I don't like it? What if this demand that I try a caper sauce infringes on my delicate taste buds and ruins my salmon? What then?"

Creepy Jack Carter was loosening up a little, and she intended to pat herself on the back for it. "If it ruins your delicate taste buds, I will order you a pizza. Because I know full well that if you don't like it, you will probably put up a bigger wall than the one around you now, and never come out of your room again." She arched a brow.

"You think I have a wall up?" he asked curiously.

"*Huge.*" She held her hand up as high as she could. She waited for him to deny it, but he didn't. He actually smiled at her.

"If I have to build a big, beautiful wall around me because of your caper sauce, you're paying for it," he said.

Whitney laughed. She opened the jar. "By the way, have you thought about ordering from the vegetarian menu? We have some great selections."

"Oh my God, what have I done?" Jack slid onto a barstool, his hands clasped before him, the hint of the smile still there.

And he was gorgeous. He was the cover of *GQ*, a romantic lead, and all the things that made her heart do loop-de-loops. She didn't know how, but Whitney was pretty sure that she might have possibly, potentially, befriended this super-handsome, super-strange and interesting man.

Seven

Jack sees a woman in a burqa walking in the midst of three little kids who have big hazel eyes and bright smiles. He knows them—they come this way every day on their way to the market. He gives them candy. He makes a show of giving it to them, holding out his fists, making them guess which hand has the candy, then divvying it up between them. They walk down the street, smiling.

A car horn sounds. There are always car horns here, but this one is different—long and urgent. Jack suddenly remembers a bomb is about to explode. He remembers because he has been here before, in this very place. He shouts at the woman to get her to turn around, but she doesn't hear him. He tries to move, to run after her, but his legs won't work. The bomb detonates and everything is black and his leg is on fire. When he looks down, he is covered with the hazel eyes of those three little kids.

Jack sat up with a shout, beating at his torso and his legs, trying to get the children's eyes off him. The air had been snatched from his lungs and he couldn't draw his breath. He frantically slapped at the covers, eyes everywhere, but it wasn't until Buster put his paws on the edge of the bed, his tail wagging, and touched Jack's arm with his wet nose that Jack remembered where he was.

He let out the breath he'd been holding and rubbed his face. Then he leaned over for Buster, dragging him onto the bed with him. Buster licked his face, turned around twice, then settled in beside Jack, his body, warm and solid, pressed against Jack's ribs.

Jack lay there in the dark. His heart raced painfully, rivulets of sweat sliding from his forehead and neck into his hairline. It was useless to try to stop seeing the scene from that day—he knew from experience that the images flooding his thoughts would not go away without help.

He feared he'd never be able to cope with it. That suicide bomber, the first one to strike the market that day, had blown the US Marines-armored Humvee to pieces. A second suicide bomber had detonated four minutes later at the other end of the open market. Jack was nowhere near the Humvee, and yet he was still knocked across the street, slamming into the corrugated siding of a small bodega as some piece of metal embedded itself in his leg. The force had caused him to pass out for a moment or two, and when he came to, he saw nothing but carnage around him.

Forty people lost their lives with the first blast, including the mother and her three children, with the candy still in their hands. Another twelve souls were lost in the second blast, including two US Marines.

In all that chaos, minutes had gone by before Jack heard his radio. He remembered how hard it was to pick himself up, to gather his wits. He remembered searching blindly around for his assault rifle and finding it nearby. When he had it in his hands, he used it to stand on one leg—and he looked at all the unfamiliar faces swirling around him. And suddenly, everyone was a bomber. Men, women, and children fleeing the scene, or rushing in to help, were bombers. He sighted his gun on person after person, suspecting everyone, his arm shaking. He frantically debated whether he should pull the trigger, or whether he was letting them all get away.

Someone grabbed him, made him lower his gun, then dragged him away and bandaged his leg. They got him out of the chaos, and though he was badly shaken and hurt, Jack thought that would be the end of it.

It wasn't.

At first, it was the recollection of that day that kept coming to him in the middle of the night, or in the middle of a task. Or he would recall a new, unshrouded detail of the day—like the smell of roasted lamb and cigarette smoke in the air. The hot, dry beat of the sun against his uniform. The steady trickle of sweat down his back.

Over time, Jack's brain began to alter his recollections. It was as if part of his brain couldn't distinguish between what had happened and the fear that something like that could happen again.

Even now, his heart was a jackhammer in his chest, unwilling to let the nightmare go. He sat up. His sheets were soaked with sweat. *Jesus, help me.* He swung his legs over the side and looked at the clock. It was three in the morning. *Great.*

Jack padded into his bathroom, opened up the medicine cabinet, and took out one of the orange pill bottles. He was supposed to take them when he couldn't calm his panic attacks. He was supposed to take the pills in the other bottle every day. He rarely took them. He was afraid of dependency. He was afraid of side effects. And he hated having to take pills—they made him feel weak. When he confessed he wasn't taking them to Dr. Pratt, she'd tried to convince him he'd make greater progress with medicinal help.

"Nah," he'd said. "I'm good." Because America was a great country, and he had everything he needed. All he needed was a promise of hope that he would not turn into Peter.

Peter Rangel had also been in that market on the day of the suicide bombers. Only he'd been at the top end of the market and he'd been wounded badly enough to warrant being honorably discharged. He'd ended up in Seattle before Jack's tour ended.

Nine months ago, Peter had taken his life.

Jack didn't know Peter had been in Seattle until Terrence Washington, another Marine buddy of his, had seen Jack's byline on a military blog and had gotten in touch. "Did you hear about Peter?" he'd asked. When Jack said no, Terrence said, "Listen, I'm going to be in Seattle tomorrow. Can we meet?"

Jack hadn't been as bad as he was now—he wasn't sure when, exactly, leaving his house had become so damn hard—and he'd met Terrence in a little café near the waterfront he knew about. Sure, he sat with his back to a wall, with a line of sight to escape, and where he could see everyone who came and went.

Terrence had sat across from him with a half-eaten burger on his plate and said, "Man, Peter killed himself last week. Stuck a Glock up under his chin."

Jack had recoiled with shock and disbelief.

According to Terrence, who'd kept in close touch with Peter, after the discharge his friend was having trouble dealing with stuff. When he started having suicidal thoughts, he'd tried to get mental health counseling from a Veterans' Administration contract clinic—Victory Health Services—but they couldn't get him in for six months. When at last he saw a psychiatrist, Terrence said, "They doped him up, man. But he didn't feel better. He felt worse."

Jack thought of the warning on his own stash of orange bottle of pills. *May cause confusion, hallucinations, or changes in behavior. May lead to thoughts of suicide or hurting yourself...*

Terrence said that Peter tried to go back to the clinic, and they scheduled him four months out. In the meantime, Peter felt so weird that he stopped taking the medicine. "Cold turkey," Terrence said. That was another warning Jack had been given—not to stop taking any medicine without a doctor's supervision, as a sudden decrease in dosage could cause a worsening of symptoms and side effects. Peter, as it turned out, was a case study of all those warnings that come with psychoactive drugs—his suicide ideation increased and he took his own life before he could make it to the follow-up appointment.

What Terrence told Jack that afternoon had shaken him to his core. Personally, he'd never had suicidal thoughts; his posttraumatic stress seemed to be another animal entirely. Nonetheless, he understood how thin the line was that separated him from Peter. How quickly he could *become* Peter.

"Here's the thing," Terrence had said, leaning across the little bistro table. "I called that clinic to tell them what they'd done, you know? I couldn't get anywhere with them. So, I drove up from Portland and went in there. I told them what happened, and how it was their fault because they wouldn't get him in. And this lady behind the counter, she pulls up this computer screen and says, see? Peter missed his appointments. But there was this other lady there, and she wouldn't look me in the eye, Jack. She turned red and she wouldn't look me in the eye. Peter didn't miss his appointment—I know because he told me. He was *upset*, man. He knew he needed help."

"Could he have mixed the days up?" Jack had asked.

Terrence shook his head. "He was texting me when this was happening. He didn't miss his appointments, Jack. I don't know how they messed up, but they did."

What Terrence wanted was someone, anyone, to do something about what had happened to his good friend Peter.

So, Jack had begun to dig in between his other assignments.

Just like Terrence said, the clinic had records that completely contradicted the texts and emails between Terrence and Peter. The clinic administration gave Jack a printout of appointment records that indicated he'd not shown up for follow-up appointments. Jack was hitting some brick walls, and thought he was going to have to give up, but then Terrence pulled an ace out of his sleeve. He talked to the woman who wouldn't look him in the eye. She'd agreed to speak with Jack, and she was the one who had called the day Christie showed up and scared him half to death.

Jack was thinking of Peter when he tossed the pill he'd been holding down his throat. He took a shower and thought about going back to bed, but the pill he'd taken had the weird effect of making him feel as though he were floating off into oblivion but making him too jittery to close his eyes. He went to work on his article about Peter with Buster curled at his feet, snoring like a two-hundred-and-fifty-pound man.

The familiar knocks and pings of his fridge startled Jack and he awoke with a start.

He'd fallen asleep in his office chair. He sat up, pushed both hands through his hair, then rubbed his face. He slowly became aware of another presence in the room. He moved his hands from his face and turned his head. Buster sat facing him, his eyes fixed on Jack, his tail slowly swishing.

Buster.

He hadn't fed his dog. He hadn't taken him out. "You hungry, buddy?" He stood, wincing—his leg was always stiff and sore in the morning. Scratching the dog's belly, he stumbled down the hallway to the kitchen. He caught sight of himself in the glass of the microwave as he poured the kibble into Buster's bowl. He looked as if he'd been out on an all-nighter. His hair stood on end. When he leaned closer, his eyes had the droopy red-rimmed look of a pothead.

Buster finished his kibble like a canine vacuum, then trotted to the door to wait. "Hold on," Jack said, which, in light of the fact it was almost one in the afternoon, was an unreasonable request to make of his dog. He searched around for shoes, shrugged into a jacket, then went into the laundry room and got Buster's raincoat and leash.

Buster was excited, clearly ready for great things to happen. He kept dancing around as Jack put his doggie raincoat on him.

The center courtyard of Jack's building could be reached by getting off at the second floor, then walking down the back flight of steps. From the courtyard, through the wrought-iron fence that kept the homeless and dog walkers who did not belong to this building from coming in, he could see the street.

At one end of the fence was the lobby where Frank spent weekdays manning the doors. On the other end of the fence was the Coffee Corner. On those occasions Jack actually made it into the Coffee Corner, he reached it by following this back route and entering a code onto a keypad so he could walk through the gate.

He eyed the coffee shop while Buster sniffed around. He could see the silhouettes of a few people inside, hunched over their laptops, big cups of coffee drinks at their elbows. That's what he used to do— there was a time he could take his laptop into any coffee shop and work all afternoon, as recently as a year or so ago. "You could do that," he muttered as he watched a couple enter the Coffee Corner. "You *invented* that, man."

Okay, he was resolved to make it to the coffee shop today. That would be twice in one week, and for a guy like him, that was entering Olympic gold medal territory.

But when he took Buster back upstairs and started to head back outside to the coffee shop, he was already swallowing down a flutter of nerves. "What's the worst that can happen?" he asked himself, as Dr. Pratt had instructed him to do. "Nothing, man. Don't be such a pussy." He made himself walk out the door and to the elevator.

As he waited for the elevator to make its appearance, his mind began to review all the possible scenarios of what could go wrong. The elevator dinged at him and the doors slid open. A guy stood there, his backpack loosely slung over his shoulder. He looked at Jack, unsmiling.

"Sorry," Jack muttered. "Forgot something." He practically jogged down the hall back to his apartment.

Once he was safely inside, he bent over at the knees and took deep breaths. "I didn't prepare," he announced breathlessly, excusing himself. "I have to prepare." He had to give himself the pep talk, had to go over all possibilities. He had to do so many things just to go downstairs and get a damn cup of coffee. Jack slid down onto his rump and covered his face with his hands.

Uncontrollable tears, thick and hot, leaked out of his eyes. Buster lay beside him and put his head in his lap. But Buster didn't get it. How was it possible that a grown ass man could be so deathly afraid of going outside? It had all come down to this—he was a shadow of the man he'd been. But he'd survived the blast! He should be celebrating that close call, but no, it ate away at him like acid, reducing him a little more each day until there was going to be nothing left of him, and then...*then*, what would he do?

He didn't like the thoughts that sprung into his head from nowhere, as if they'd been lurking in the weeds of his thoughts, waiting to strike. Thoughts that went something along the lines of ending up like Peter. It shook him. Jack remembered that Dr. Pratt had told him he should call any time he was having trouble.

He lifted his head, hugged Buster, then got up off the floor and wiped his face with the back of his hand. He went to his office and called. Ten minutes later, Dr. Pratt Skyped him.

"Well, hello, Jack," she said when he answered. "I wasn't expecting to speak to you today."

"You said I should call if…" He shrugged.

"That's right. What would you like to talk about?"

"Nothing." He realized how stupid that sounded. He hadn't interrupted her day with nothing to talk about. "I mean, I, ah…" He nervously shoved a hand through his hair. "I wanted to report a couple of things."

"Okay." She was smiling. She always smiled. In some ways, she reminded him of his mother. His mother was always patient, like Dr. Pratt. But Dr. Pratt understood him. His mother couldn't drive because she was afraid of highways.

"Well, I tried a new sauce last night that the dinner girl made," he said, because that was fairly big news in his world, when one was concerned about being poisoned, and it was easier to tell her that than the fact that he'd been crying at his inability to get a cup of coffee fifteen minutes ago. "It was pretty good."

"That's *great*," Dr. Pratt said cheerfully. "Did she

suggest it?"

He nodded. "She brought it. She said..." He couldn't help a small smile. "She said I lacked diversity. And then she gave me a list of vegetarian meal kits to order."

"You agreed with her that you should branch out? That's exciting, Jack. Have you ordered them?"

"No," he said. "I need to study them."

"Why?"

He gave her a look. Dr. Pratt liked it when he admitted his weaknesses, even though she knew them all as well as he did. "You *know* why, doc."

"Remind me," she said, as if she'd forgotten everything about the last few months.

"Because I need to know the ingredients."

"As I recall, one of the reasons you picked this service was because the cook did the shopping. That would mean your friend would be the one to purchase the ingredients, since she does the shopping. I think you can assume, given your experience thus far, that she will be careful. Why don't you invite your friend to have supper with you? That should solve any lingering doubts," she suggested.

Eat with her? "Whoa," he said. That was too much, too soon. He'd just *met* her. "I don't...I'm not sure—"

"You might feel more comfortable trying something new if you had a friend try it with you. Remember, you need to identify portals to safety. Having someone you trust to eat the same foods as you can help you feel safe and can help you progress."

"I don't know." He needed to think about it.

Dr. Pratt cocked her head to one side. "Have you been taking your med—"

"No," he said quickly before she gave him a lecture about it. "Once," he amended. "Last night."

"Nightmare?"

He nodded. He shoved his hand through his hair and looked away for a moment.

"Your anxiety about something like this would be significantly reduced if you took what I've prescribed, Jack," she said patiently.

"That's okay. I'm fine. Really. I'm fine."

"Did you go to the coffee shop today?"

He was actually squirming in his seat. He couldn't tell her—it was too humiliating. "I got a late start today."

She nodded. "I think you should ask yourself why you haven't left your apartment in so long if you're truly as fine as you claim."

Jack clamped his mouth shut. He didn't want to say what was in his head. He didn't want to shout that *she* didn't have a buddy who killed himself after taking those pills—*he* did. And furthermore, suicide bombers were everywhere, hello.

Dr. Pratt looked at something to the side. "I have an appointment in a few minutes. When will your friend be back?"

"I wouldn't exactly call her my friend. More like… my cook," he said, although that didn't sound right, either.

"Let's think of her as your friend."

"Let's not," Jack said.

"When will she be back?"

"Tomorrow."

"Great!" She jotted something down. "My challenge to you before our next session is to try the coffee shop again. And I'd like you to invite your friend to have dinner with you, in your house, eating the same food you're eating. Then we'll talk about how all that went."

Jack's mind was already starting to turn over on itself. So many thoughts crowded into his head.

"You can do it, Jack. Logically, you know that nothing is going to happen. You know the ingredients are safe. You just have to keep reminding yourself of that. We'll talk on Monday, all right? Take your medicine," she said, and with a wink, clicked off.

Jack spent the remainder of the day churning over her instructions for him.

He attempted to take his mind off the anxiety by trying Terrence's source in the clinic again and finally, *finally,* got her to call him back again. "I can't talk now," was all she said when he explained who he was.

"Can I call you Saturday, Sharon?" he asked. "Is that okay? Maybe it's better if we talk when you're not at work."

"I don't know. That doesn't sound like a good idea. I have to go—"

"Don't hang up," he begged her. "Listen, I wouldn't bother you if it wasn't important. But Peter...Peter *killed* himself, Sharon, and I don't want that to happen to anyone else. I'm a journalist, and I swear on Peter's life I will never reveal your name to anyone."

There was a long silence until she said, "Okay. Call me at eleven on Saturday." She hung up.

That small diversion didn't last long. Jack's anxiety began to creep back in. He did not make it to the coffee shop, but he did order a vegetarian meal from Dinner Magic. He agonized about it, studying them, and decided he could live with the chickpea and couscous casserole, which had no sauce that he could determine—sauce being notoriously easy to poison—and included things in cans, which were notoriously hard to poison.

At then, at last, several hours later, it was Friday. He was, he realized, a bit excited. He wanted to see Whitney again. He wanted to see her pretty blue eyes, her curvy figure. He wanted the smile to wash over him again.

Buster was excited, too, particularly when Rain showed up to take him to the dog park. His dog greeted the hipster ex-Marine as though he were his long-lost brother.

It should have been Jack taking Buster to the dog park. It should have been Jack all along. A surge of righteous indignation raced through his veins as he watched Buster trot away with Rain. He was going to beat this. He was going to fight off this anxiety and return to the guy he was, and if he didn't, he would literally die trying.

When Buster and Rain had gone, Jack swept up his keys and marched to the elevator, hitting the down button several times, grateful that it arrived before he could chicken out. He was going to man up. He would go to Coffee Corner, goddammit, and he would get a coffee and a bagel. And then, he was going to ask Whitney to stay for dinner.

Eight

Whitney finally got smart and purchased an insulated rolling cooler to carry her client's groceries and her baked goods. She was feeling pretty smug about her purchase and how well organized she could be when she wanted to...until she tried to maneuver the thing into the very crowded Coffee Corner. It had started to rain on a Friday afternoon, which meant insanity prevailed inside. Across Seattle, entire office buildings emptied out into coffeehouses on rainy Friday afternoons.

A random guy was nice enough to hold the door open for her so she could wheel her cooler inside. The thing now looked like a monstrosity, taking up as much space as a chair. The same helpful guy darted in front of her to get in line, having done his good deed for the day. Unfortunately, he had the look of one of those office workers dispatched to bring back a half dozen frozen coffee drinks to the team meeting.

As it was, the line to the counter was to the damn door. Whitney inched along, nudging her cooler in front of her as if it were a child. She texted her sister Taylor to pass the time, but that made things worse, because Taylor told her their father was planning to come to Seattle. She clicked off her phone and shoved it into her jacket pocket. The last thing she needed was for Dad to show up and do the old I-told-you-so business.

"Hey," said a girl behind her. "Your turn."

Whitney pushed her cooler forward to the counter. The clerk at the register wore a head covering and a gold nose ring. "Hi, Farida," Whitney said. "What's up?"

"The usual. What's up with you?" Farida asked.

"I've got cakes, that's what. Is Ben around?" Whitney asked, referring to the manager.

"Yep. I'll let him know you're here. Do you want something to drink?"

Whitney waved her off and stepped to the side as Farida disappeared through a door. She returned a moment later. "He's on the phone and said to hang a minute."

Whitney maneuvered around two men waiting for their coffees and squeezed past the display case. Someone was standing in the corner near the hallway to the bathroom, shoved up against the wall as if he were hiding. He had his back to her, but Whitney recognized that back. She stepped forward and tapped him on the shoulder. "Hey!"

Jack jerked around with such force that his coffee went flying, spilling onto the side of the display case, his jacket, the floor, and onto the purse Whitney carried on her shoulder. "*Shit,*" he hissed.

"God, I'm so sorry." Whitney looked down at the spill spreading on the floor. "I scared you."

"I wasn't *scared,*" he said quickly.

"I mean, I startled you." Scared, startled—she'd definitely given him a fright. She grabbed a stack of napkins off the condiments bar, threw several onto the floor to stop the spill from spreading any more, then pressed a few up against his chest.

Jack gasped and recoiled.

"What?" Whitney demanded, slightly annoyed. "You're dripping coffee."

Jack glanced down. "Right," he said. "Right, right." He covered her hand with his to take the napkins from her.

In certain circumstances, Whitney was prone to reading too much into a simple gesture or a quick look. But for a teeny moment, she felt a charge shock through her when Jack's hand covered hers. He must have felt it, too, because he didn't move his hand or take the napkins—they were both frozen. When he realized he was holding her hand, he moved quickly to snatch the napkins.

Whitney grabbed more napkins from the condiment bar and soaked up the bit of coffee on her purse.

"I'm really sorry." He squatted down to mop up the spill.

"It's okay! Accidents happen."

He nodded, stood, and dumped the wad of napkins into the trash. She noticed a bead of perspiration sliding down his temple. He swiped the back of his hand across his forehead as if the act of wiping up the mess had been strenuous.

"Would you like another coffee?" Whitney asked.

Jack glanced at the line and swallowed. "Ah...no. There are a lot of people in here." He shoved his hands into his pockets.

"Yes, but I have connections." She leaned across the display case. "Hey, Farida? Can you get this guy another drink? I made him spill his coffee." She glanced back at Jack. "What do you want?"

Jack stared at her. Then he stared at Farida.

"Coffee, right?" Farida said. "Black?"

Jack nodded.

Farida poured him another coffee, but when she attempted to hand it to him, he just stared at the cup. What was wrong with him? Was he having a seizure? Whitney quickly intervened and took the coffee. "Thanks, I owe you," she said to Farida. She turned around to hand the coffee to Jack.

He looked at Whitney.

"It's coffee," she said. "Are you all right?"

He finally lifted his hand, and when he did, she noticed the slight tremble in it. A million things ran through her mind, but drugs and alcohol were at the top of her list. Who else trembled like that? Just great—she'd taken interest in an addict. She slowly lifted her gaze to his.

"I know, I look like a drunk," he said bitterly, and took the coffee.

Was it her imagination, or was he perspiring more now? "A little," she admitted. "Or like you're coming down from something. Are you?"

"*No*," he said, and noticing her skepticism, "I swear it, Whitney. It's just...I've been having trouble sleeping."

She wasn't convinced. But she reasoned that if he had a drinking problem, she would have seen signs of it. Like lots of empty bottles in the trash. And there was a bottle of wine that had been sitting on his counter for weeks, untouched. Was it drugs? Jesus— she didn't know anyone who did drugs. "Why can't you sleep?" she asked curiously.

"I'm working on an important article. Too much coffee, I guess." He tried to give her a sheepish smile, but he simply looked miserable.

She decided then and there that she'd give him the benefit of the doubt. He was terribly awkward, and something didn't quite add up, but still, she felt sorry for him. "Hey!" she said suddenly. "You ordered a vegetarian kit!"

He shifted his gaze to his coffee. "I'm going to give it a chance."

She laughed. "A chance? While I commend you for walking out on the limb of couscous and chickpeas, you don't have to enter into a committed relationship with them. Anyway, you're going to *love* it."

"Whitney?"

She turned around. Ben, the regional manager, had appeared on the other side of the display case in all his bearded glory. He adjusted his wire-rimmed glasses. "Hi, Ben!" she said, forgetting about Jack for the moment. "Look what I've got for you today." She opened her insulated tote and removed one of her mini cakes. "It's four hundred and fifty calories. This one is chocolate. I've also got vanilla, caramel, and my personal favorite, strawberry."

"*Nice.*" He nodded approvingly as she held up the cake. "A music box, huh?"

"Yep." She slid the cake onto the case, pulled out another one and set it beside the first. "This is just a small sample of what you could expect."

"Awesome," he said. "Well, the team is on board." He picked up one of the cakes to have a look. "They've sold fast and we think they're fantastic. We'd love to carry them."

Whitney gasped with delight. "That's fantastic!" Coffee Corner had three stores downtown. This was the sort of opportunity she'd been working so hard to achieve.

"All we need is your health department certificate, a complete list of ingredients and ingredient sources, and a schedule of delivery. Delivery day-of is better than day-before if you can swing it. We can work out quantities."

He was talking, but Whitney was stuck on the first thing he'd said. *Health department*. She could feel her elation leaking out of her like air from a balloon. "Ah," she said.

"What?" Ben asked her. "Is something wrong?"

"I don't have the health department certificate just yet," she said. That was fudging the truth—she couldn't get the certificate to distribute baked goods commercially without a proper commercial kitchen. No health department inspector would approve the stupid little kitchen in the stupid little studio she'd rented. "I'm working on it."

"Oh," Ben said. "That sucks." He looked at the cakes. "Afraid my hands are tied—I can't carry your cakes without the certificate."

"Right, right." She waved a hand at him. "I totally get it. I should have it any time now. *Government*." She rolled her eyes.

"Awful," he agreed. "Well, look, come back when you've got it. Want a coffee?" He jerked his thumb over his shoulder. "It's on the house."

"Thanks, but no." She forced a cheerful smile. "I've got a job I have to get to. Keep the cakes for the staff, okay?"

Ben thanked her and took the cakes. She zipped up her cooler, stood up...and looked right into Jack's eyes. Wonderful. She'd forgotten he was there to witness her failure.

"Hey," he said. The coffee was gone, and his hands were shoved deep into his pockets again. "Want to get out of here?"

She smiled with surprise. It seemed a little sudden, but what was he asking her, exactly? Not that, apparently, because he looked as if he were going to choke.

"I mean...you're making dinner anyway, so you might as well come up."

Ah. So it was that kind of question, the *when will my dinner be ready* kind of question. "Sure." She now felt defeated on all possible fronts.

They went out of the coffee shop, him with his hands shoved so deep in his pockets she thought he might be able to tie his shoes from there, and her dragging her stupid cooler behind her.

But when they reached the door to his apartment building, he inadvertently put his hand to the small of her back and got the door, and she not-so-inadvertently brushed against him, and he felt hard and lean and sort of soft at the same time, and Whitney all at once forgot the health department.

Nine

For a few moments in that coffee shop, Jack forgot about all the potential danger because he was taken aback by how dejected Whitney had looked. He didn't know anything about the ins and outs of the bakery business, but he knew something was wrong.

She was in his kitchen now, puttering around without her usual energy, seemingly distracted. She didn't seem to realize he was here, leaning against the wall, his arms folded tightly across his chest. She was wearing a white button-up blouse, a plaid skirt, some black tights, and military boots. She couldn't have looked any cuter if she'd tried, and Jack was trying not to let his mind go down the path of seeing those clothes peel off her, one by one. He tried to think of something to say that didn't sound ridiculously out of touch—or worse, stupid.

He watched her mix ingredients in a large mixing bowl.

She glanced at his kitchen clock. "I'm a little early," she said. "I'll bake it, and you can keep it in the oven to stay warm until you're ready."

Jack nodded.

She sighed, as if his lack of response had disappointed her. Well, he couldn't say anything—his thoughts and tongue were all tied up in how to ask her to have dinner with him. Such a simple question! How hard could it be? How badly could he screw it up?

"Any big plans for the weekend?" She sounded almost morose about it.

"No." *Speak, idiot! Tell her something! Like what? That I'll probably be curled up in a corner somewhere because someone honked a horn?*

The door suddenly swung open and in bounded Buster, panting loudly. He was wet, his feet muddy.

"Hey, hey!" Rain said after him. "He wouldn't let me wipe off his feet, man!" He held up a towel.

"I've got it." Jack took the towel from Rain. He squatted down to greet his dog and wipe off his feet.

"Hey, Whitney!" Rain said as he passed through the kitchen to return Buster's leash to the laundry room.

"Oh, hi, Rain."

At the sound of her voice, Buster wiggled free of Jack and raced into the kitchen, colliding with an open cabinet door in his haste. Whitney laughed. God, but Jack loved the sound of her laugh. It made all the difference in the somber mood that had pervaded his house just moments ago. "Did you miss me? I know what you want, you little chow hound." She reached across the bar into her bag. She tossed Buster a treat and laughed when he caught it and all but swallowed it whole.

Rain reappeared and propped his elbows on the bar. "Girl. I gotta tell you—that was one unbelievable cupcake."

"Thanks!" she said.

"I mean, it was *perfect*, man. You should, like, totally set up shop downstairs and sell them."

"Yep, I should," she said. "Here, have a mini cake." She dipped down into the big rolling cooler and handed him one of her music box cakes.

"Seriously?" Rain said. "You sure?"

"I've never been more sure. Enjoy." She fluttered the fingers of both hands at him before she turned back to her bowl.

"*Awesome*," Rain said. "Thanks!" He held it up like a trophy to Jack. "I'll see you Sunday, all right, Buster?"

Buster responded by melting down onto the kitchen floor.

Rain walked past Jack, grinning. "*Cake*, man."

"Cake," Jack agreed, and watched Rain go out. He stepped up to the bar and said, "So…this health department thing."

"Yep, it's a problem," she said. "Not an impossible problem, but a pretty damn big one for me right now. I can't sell anything without the permit. But I can't get the permit without the commercial kitchen. And I can't get a commercial kitchen until I find a place I can afford." She sighed again. "Maybe my dad was right."

"Your dad?"

"Oh," she said, and waved a hand at him. "Don't let me get started. It's just that my dad wanted me to be a lawyer. He thinks it's a much better career path, and by the look of things, he's right."

"Yeah, but there's the whole thing about having to go to law school," Jack pointed out.

"I did that."

"You did what?"

"I went to law school."

"You're a lawyer?" he asked, confused.

"Not exactly," she said. "I graduated from law school, but I didn't take the bar exam."

"Why not?"

"Well, because I was miserable. I'd been miserable for three years of law school, and the four years of pre-law as an undergraduate, and there I was, twenty-eight years old, hating what I'd set my life up to be." She paused in her mixing to look at him. "Can you even imagine what that's like?"

Yeah, he could imagine what it was like to be something you hated.

"Anyway, I was studying for the bar and I woke up one day and had this epiphany. I told my parents I hated law, I have always hated it, and I was going to be a baker. A real baker, like one who could get a show on the Food Network, you know?"

Well no, he didn't know, but he'd go with it.

"So, over the objections of my entire family—my parents, my sister, who is already practicing law in my dad's firm, and my brother, a heart doctor, and various aunts and uncles—I took the money I inherited from my grandmother and moved to Seattle to start this fabulous bakery. But I can't seem to find a place that I can renovate and afford. *Dammit*." She cracked the spoon against the bowl. "Sorry," she added sheepishly, and began to stir the contents of the bowl with a vengeance.

Jack tried to think of something to say. He ran

several things through his head, but they all sounded like tired clichés. *Just keep trying,* or *Never say never.* He watched her pour the casserole into a pan.

"Do you want me to put this in the oven?" she asked.

"What?" He was exasperated by his inability to say something meaningful to her.

"The casserole." She frowned a little, probably exasperated with his inability, too. "Do you want me to put it in the oven," she said again, articulating clearly. "I can bake it now if you like, but it's only four."

"Sure," he said. "I'll warm it later."

Her brows dipped. "I'm not supposed to go off without baking and plating your dish."

"I seem to recall this conversation from two days ago," he said.

"They haven't changed the rules in the last two days."

"It's okay," he said. "I can turn on an oven and I promise I won't report you."

She gave him a very pretty, very wry little smile. "You promise?" She took off her apron. "Well then, I'll get out of your hair."

She began to pack up her things. Jack stood there at the bar like a mannequin. He was desperate to ask her to stay. He tried to make his tongue work, but it suddenly felt as if he had swallowed a wad of cotton. Even Buster lifted his head and gave him a plaintive look. *What are you doing? Why is this so hard?*

Whitney quickly had her things together and picked up her purse and slung it over her shoulder. "Okay, I guess I'll see you next week. Hope you like the couscous and your taste buds aren't ruined." She smiled again, then started toward the door, rolling the cooler behind her.

Buster leaped up and trotted after her.

She was about to walk out the door. She was about to leave and he couldn't ask her the simplest question.

"*Whitney!*" Jesus, did he actually just shout her name? He must have, because she sort of whipped around. Jack shoved his hands into his pockets. *Come on, come on…*

"Yes?"

"I, ah… I'm…" He tried to swallow the cottony thing in his throat. He must look like an imbecile to her.

"You're what?" she asked impatiently.

"Will you eat with me." Regrettably, he did not present it as a question. It was a rushed, practiced statement that sounded so bizarre it was a wonder she didn't bolt through the door.

Her brows dipped, and she stared at him, clearly trying to work it out.

He released a big breath he didn't realize he'd been holding, annoyed by how much energy it took to ask an attractive woman to dinner. "Dinner," he croaked. "I mean, if you want to. You don't have to. You probably have stuff to do. Friends, or baking, something, I don't know. Look, I'm sorry I said anything. I shouldn't have asked. My bad."

Whitney's mouth gaped a bit. Then she said, "*Wow.* That was a spectacularly bad invitation."

He cringed. "I'm sorry."

"I don't know if you want me to eat with you or not." She sounded more curious than offended. "Do you?"

He nodded. "Yes, I do."

Whitney suddenly smiled, and the warmth of it shifted the mood in the narrow little hallway.

Jack suddenly didn't feel so stupid. He felt pretty damn good.

"Yes, Jack, I will eat with you. I don't know why, because you're a little kooky, but yes, I will. Would you like me to come back later after you've turned on the oven?"

"Okay." That was not what he'd meant, but he'd go with whatever she wanted.

"That was a joke." She shoved her rolling cooler by the door and shrugged out of her jacket. "I am not going out in the rain for an hour just to come back. You'll just have to put up with me. I mean seriously, what is *wrong* with you?" She smiled, and gave him a playful little push as she walked past him and into his apartment.

Buster, made incredibly happy by this turn of events, woofed at her. Jack would have woofed, too, if he hadn't been so damn nervous.

"I know, buddy, I know," she said soothingly to his dog. "Things are just a little weird up in here." She glanced over her shoulder at Jack, her eyes sparkling. "But I kind of like it."

Ten

"**I** think we should open that bottle of wine," Whitney suggested. She stood in Jack's kitchen again, her hands on her hips, surveying the lay of the land. Uptight Ernie was going to need a little help loosening up, seeing as how he could hardly hold it together to ask her to stay. His fumbling of it had endeared him to her, but she was not going to spend the evening dragging each and every word out of him.

"That wine has been there for three months," Jack said.

"Then it should be perfectly aged." She arched a brow at him, daring him to disagree.

He looked at the wine.

"What's the matter, you don't drink?" She opened a drawer for a wine opener. She knew where everything was in his kitchen.

"I drink," he said. "Or I did. I guess I've been kind of tied up in a piece I'm working on and haven't had a drink in a while."

"You ought to get out more," she said.

He pressed his lips together. "Yeah, I should."

"This must be some piece or whatever that you're working on." She removed the foil from the top of the wine bottle.

"It is," he agreed. He still stood at the wall, his back pressed against it.

If he wasn't going to talk, this could very well be the longest dinner of her life. "Were you always going to be a writer?" she asked in an attempt to rev the conversation.

"Never crossed my mind. I wanted to be a Marine." He looked at his hand. "So when I finished college, I went into the service. I figured out the writing thing later."

"A Marine, huh?" Whitney said, impressed.

"Yep."

She waited for him to say more, but of course he didn't. "Okay, I'll bite—where were you a Marine? Here? Overseas? In your backyard?"

"My backyard…what? No. I served two tours of duty in Afghanistan."

"*Oh*." She popped the cork and looked at him. "That sounds heavy."

He shrugged.

"Is that where you got the limp?"

He looked surprised, as if he didn't know it was an obvious limp. "Yeah," he said. "Took some shrapnel." He gestured lamely at his leg then shifted his gaze to the window.

It didn't take a savant to see that his leg was a sore subject for him. "How long have you been out?" she asked.

"Two years."

She poured two glasses of wine and set them on the bar. She went to the fridge and removed a block of cheese she knew was in there. It was weird, being so familiar with a man's kitchen and not so familiar with him. She put the cheese on a plate, added some grapes, and some nuts from the pantry, and placed them on the bar. She looked up at Jack, who watched her with a look of amazement.

"Do you mind? You have like three bricks of cheese in there, and a drawer full of grapes." She walked around to take a seat at the bar.

"I'm on grocery delivery." He smiled a little. "You probably won't be surprised to know that I order the same thing every week."

She laughed and slid onto a bar seat. "You're right, I'm not."

Jack remained at the wall. She gestured to the barstool beside her. "Am I that scary? I promise not to attack you."

His eyes widened for a breath of a moment, but then a smile slowly spread across his face. "You're not that scary." He pushed away from the wall and walked with that slight limp to take a seat beside her.

Whitney twirled around to face him. She picked up her wine glass, motioned for him to do the same, and clinked her glass to his. "To new friends."

"Are we friends?" he asked.

"Don't overthink it, just drink."

He drank. He drank a lot. He drank that wine as if it were water. He drained the glass and she poured him more.

"And you sure you're not an alcoholic?" she teased him.

"Wasn't until today," he said, and his smile deepened to a point where Whitney could imagine swimming in it. It made her feel tingly. He had awesome brown eyes, glittery and inviting. His lips were full and delectable, and feelings stirred in her that she was sure Scaredycat Sam would not like.

She drank some wine, then popped a grape in her mouth. "Okay, you came back to Seattle when you left the Marines, right?"

"Right."

"Are you from Seattle?"

"No," he said. "Eagle's Ridge. Do you know it?"

She shook her head.

"It's a couple of hours from here, a small town in the Blue Mountains."

"Aha," Whitney said.

"Aha?"

"Aha, you're from a small town. The photo of those boys on your shelf looks like a small-town picture."

He looked over his shoulder at the photos on his shelves.

"Eagle's Ridge, right? Which one are you?" She hopped off her stool to fetch the photo.

When she returned with it, Jack pointed to a kid with a crooked smile, a dark mop of hair, and a black eye. "Had a fight that day," he said. "Fists swinging, legs kicking, the whole nine yards."

"About what?"

"A girl, what else?"

Whitney laughed. "Look at you." She touched the frame. "You look like trouble." He looked so cute. He looked pissed.

"I *was* trouble," he said. "That picture was taken

in detention. Those are my best friends." He pointed them out. "That's Noah. He kicked my ass that day because Lainey broke up with me." He chuckled. "She's Noah's cousin, and he thought I'd dumped her." He gave Whitney a sidelong look. "I had a reputation," he said sheepishly. "But the truth was that Lainey dumped me."

"She did? What'd you do?"

"Nothing, really. But I was best friends with Noah, and she was smart enough to know that she and I were not going to work out, and if it went on too long, it would ruin our friendship."

Whitney looked at the photo again. "I guess she was too late."

"Actually, the three of us became really close. *Really* close." He swallowed. "Lainey has cancer. Noah called me up to let me know she's dying and I…" He swallowed again. He picked up his wine glass and drank. "I haven't made it back to Eagle's Ridge yet."

He felt guilt about that, she could sense it. She stared at the photo of the boys. "How long were you in detention?"

"That time? A couple of months. But we liked it," he said with a lopsided smile, and looked up, present again.

"You *liked* it?"

"The teacher was hot." He pointed at the photo. "Those pubescent boys were actively in love with her." He laughed.

Jack Carter had a warm, inviting laugh, and it was such a contrast to the man Whitney had come to know that she was both startled and titillated by it. "So where are these guys now?" she asked.

"Mostly Eagle's Ridge," he said, still studying the photo.

"What about your parents?" she asked. "Are they in Seattle?"

He shook his head. "Dad had a heart attack and died while I was in Afghanistan. Mom still lives in Eagle's Ridge. And Christie lives in the North Beach area."

"It's just you and Buster, huh?"

"Yep."

That seemed really lonely to Whitney. And a little curious, to be honest. Jack had everything going for him—he was so hot, and he was a veteran, and a writer, and he lived in a fancy downtown building and had an awesome dog. Under any other circumstance, that would be solid gold on the dating circuit. But there was something a little off about Jack. She couldn't put her finger on it, exactly. He wasn't standoffish so much as he was reserved. He wasn't flirty and handsy, either, but seemed almost afraid of touch. He was an interesting, curious man, and she wished he would relax.

She wanted to understand the current running in him—he wasn't like any man she'd ever met before.

At least he was talking now, and she liked it. Maybe the wine had loosened him up. It had loosened her up, too, and she was finding it difficult not to ogle him. His shoulders and arms filled his shirt, and she could see the curve of muscle that defined them.

She was imagining what he would look like without that shirt when he said, "Your turn," and put aside the photo of the boys. "Where'd you go to law school?"

"Ugh. Law school." She told him about UCLA,

and the family law firm, and the sprawling mansion in Orange County the Baldwin family of litigators called home.

"Why didn't you open a bakery in Orange County?"

"I looked at several places. I chose Seattle because I've always liked it, but also for the demographics and the business climate. I didn't choose Orange County because my dad does not approve." She waggled her brows. "Like, *really* doesn't approve. He wants me to fail."

"Come on," Jack said in disbelief. "What dad would want his daughter to fail? What could he possibly have against bakers?"

"Not fail, exactly," she clarified. "My dad is one of those guys who thinks whatever his children do reflects on him. He can't stand the thought of having a daughter who is making cupcakes when she could be a big important lawyer."

"That must be hard for you." His gaze had traveled upward a bit, to her hair. And then to her mouth, where he lingered.

"You have no idea." She felt a little fizzy suddenly.

"I guess I'm not the only one rattling around Seattle on my own." His gaze slipped to her neck.

"Guess not." The fizziness turned into a tiny little fire. She liked the way he was looking at her—with interest. The tension in him was changing from day to dusk. Easing. Quieting. Now she could see his hunger.

Hunger.

Whitney was reminded of the casserole and glanced at her watch. "Oops...time got away from me." She hopped off the barstool.

Jack slid off his stool, too, and suddenly, they were standing *mano-y-mano*, so close that their shirts touched. "Where are you going?" he asked.

The tiny fire in her spread and bloomed, stirring up all sorts of feelings and desires. "I have to turn on the oven," she said to his lips.

"Right now?" He touched a lock of her hair, pushed it back over her shoulder.

"It has to warm up," she said to his chest. She wanted to touch it, to lay her palm flat against it and feel the heat in his skin, the beat of his heart. The fire in her crackled and swirled in a sparkly little vortex around them. *Was he going to kiss her?* He looked as if he wanted to. She would be on board with that, and lifted her chin slightly to help.

"It warms up quick." He touched her chin, tracing a path up to her ear. "You'd be surprised how quick."

Kiss me! she shouted in her head. But Jack didn't move. He kept looking at her as though he wanted to cover her in ice cream and eat his way to the bottom, but now his hands were in his back pockets, as if he was intentionally holding himself off. What a strange, funny man he was. Whitney realized that if she had to wait for him to make the first move, she might be standing here all night. She was on the verge of bursting. So she took matters into her own hands, grabbed his head between her hands and said, "Brace yourself," and kissed him.

She thought Jack tried to pedal backward, but she wasn't going to let that happen. She put her arms around his neck, rose up on her toes, pressed against him and moved her lips on his, touching the tip of her tongue to the seam of his lips.

After a moment's hesitation, Jack grabbed her

and pulled her hard into his body. One arm encircled her waist with the strength of a steel band. His fingers splayed across her cheek and he lifted his head, his eyes searching her face. "Do you know what you're doing?" he asked roughly.

She didn't think it required explanation. "I'm kissing you."

"You get where this will probably lead."

Oh, she got it all right. "Are you in or out?" she demanded, unwilling to debate the significance of this kiss, or anything that might follow.

"So in," he said, a little breathless. "But don't ask me a lot of questions. Just go with it."

"What?"

"Trust me on this," he said.

"Okay, but—"

He would not allow a *but*. He walked her backward as he smothered her with steamy kisses, firing up all the cylinders in her that desired hot, molten sex, and moved her down the hall.

She could feel his erection between them, could feel the skin of his arms heating beneath her touch. He walked her into a bedroom, kicked the door closed behind him—"Sorry Buster," he said—and in a move that defied physics, picked her up and sort of vaulted with her through space and onto his unmade bed so hard that they bounced.

"You're not going to freak out, are you?" she asked as he began to unbutton her shirt.

"Can't make any promises," he said without missing a beat. He yanked his shirt off his body.

Jesus, Mary, and Joseph, look at him. She didn't care whether he freaked out or not—she was the one who would have a meltdown. His skin was taut over muscle, and on his right pectoral, he had a small tattoo, the symbol of the Marines with the letters *USMC*. He was a beast. A mouth-watering, sexy beast. Her body thrummed along at a little clip and she wasn't going to power down. She sat up and pulled her shirt free.

He took one look at her breasts. "My God, you're perfect." He cupped one breast, nibbled at the red lacy strap.

"No, I'm not," she said. "But say it again." She nuzzled his neck.

"You are *perfect*." He kissed the swell of her breast.

A little hyperbole in the bedroom wasn't going to hurt anyone. Frankly, Whitney was so horny and it had been so long since she'd had great sex that he could say she was a doughy muffin and she'd still be turned on. She reached for the button of his jeans, but Jack was ahead of her. He managed to unbutton them and kiss her breasts at the same time.

He kicked off his shoes and grabbed her leg, lifting one up so he could pull off a boot, and then the other. He began to slowly slide his hand up her leg; little shivers raced up her spine. "You're not hiding anything under that skirt, are you?" he asked as he reached her thigh.

"Like what?"

"Like…anything."

"I have the usual equipment," she said. "I'm not hiding a penis, if that's what you're worried about."

Jack's hand stopped moving. "A *what*? I didn't mean—"

"Forget it." She pushed up so that she could sink her fingers in his hair and kiss him.

He continued that torturous slide of his hand up her skirt. He was all soft lips and tongue, all roaming hands with a touch so hot and light at the same time that he was turning her into a quivering bowl of Jell-O. This man could do anything he wanted to her right now and she wouldn't stop him. She could feel her tights rolling off her, his hand between her legs, his fingers exploring. She slid her hands over his body, down his hips—which were bared now, for somehow, he'd managed to get all their clothes off them with the exception of her bra—and down his leg. She felt something odd and turned her head. She could now see that just above his knee, covering a good portion of his thigh, his flesh was purple and misshapen. The cause of his limp. Jack took her hand from his leg and moved it, to the soft nest of hair and the thick cock between them.

She wrapped her fingers around him and sighed. "I was going to seduce *you*," she complained.

He kissed the patch of skin behind her ear and that sent fluttering fits of desire through her. "You started it, but I'm going to finish it," he murmured. He rolled her onto her belly and began an arousing assault to her senses with his mouth on her skin, pausing to unhook her bra with his teeth—*with his teeth*—and then languidly continuing on to her hip. He rose back up, kissed the back of her neck, then rolled her over and began again, tracing another sensual path down her body, including both breasts, her belly, and settling between her legs. Sparks flew now—dangerous, explosion-inducing sparks that seemed to be firing from all her fingers and toes.

"See? I was going to do that to you, too, but you ruined it," she said between pants of pleasure. He chuckled against her thigh and continued to stroke her with his tongue. When she thought she couldn't bear it another moment, when she thought she would come apart at the seams, he rose up, groped around in a bedside table, and produced a condom.

When he was ready, he braced himself above her and gazed down at her. A moment passed. Then another. Something seemed off. Whitney came up on her elbows and pushed a bit of hair from his forehead. "What's the matter?"

"Nothing." He dipped his head. "I don't...I don't know."

What the hell was happening? Everything had been clicking along. Whitney couldn't guess what was going through his strange brain, but he was still rock hard. "Act Two." She pushed at his chest and forced him onto his back. She straddled him and slid down onto his cock before he could speak.

That was it for her. He felt perfect inside her, and she found herself floating away on a surprisingly frothy concoction of hard-bodied man, burning desire, and earthy pleasure. She moved on him as if she'd taken lessons, moving them both toward a release that she felt pretty sure might blow out the windows. Somewhere in the middle of that most excellent ride, Jack put his arm around her waist and rolled with her, putting her on her side, and taking over the work. They glided along on that surf of pure pleasure until Whitney couldn't bear it another moment and was rocked into the oblivion of physical release. She pitched forward into the sensation, pressing into his body and gave in completely to his strokes, to his kisses, to the rolling waves of pleasure that washed over her. A moment later, Jack gave in to the pull of release, too, thrusting into her one last time with a garbled moan.

Her heart pounded so hard with elation that she could hardly hear herself breathe. She rolled onto her back, still trying to catch her breath, still stunned by the amazing sensation of it all. Jack rolled onto his back, too. He was breathing just as hard as she was, his eyes closed. She sat up, kissed his chest, then crawled off the bed.

"Wait." He reached for her. "Where are you going?"

She picked up his shirt from the floor and pulled it over her head, breathing in the spicy, oaky scent. "To turn on the oven."

He came up on his elbow. "You're still going to cook?"

"Yep. It's my job, and I'm starving. Aren't you hungry? Fun fact—I am always hungry after a little toss in the hay. Like, ravenous. I don't know what that is." She pushed her hair from her face. She smiled at him, and her smile felt full of affection. Whether it was for great sex, or whether Weird Al here was growing on her, Whitney didn't precisely know.

His expression in return was not something she completely understood. He looked a little fearful, a tiny bit awestruck, and something else. He looked, she thought, a little grateful. If anyone should be grateful, it was her. She felt like the sexiest badass woman in all of Seattle right now. She wasn't sure, but she bet her hair was perfectly mussed and her lipstick was still on her mouth, and that she looked completely adorable in his shirt. *That's* how good she felt.

Eleven

That Friday afternoon romp turned into Saturday morning—Jack and Whitney had spent the evening curled up together on the couch and in his bed. Jack was very effectively reminded why he'd liked sex so much Before Afghanistan.

He was in a very good mood owing to that most excellent sex when she said she had to meet her realtor midday Saturday. He was in awe that they— *he*—had talked so much. Astoundingly, she'd broken through an invisible dam in him—he'd said more in two days than he had in the last two years. And that included his bi-weekly torturous sessions with Dr. Pratt.

What had seemed impossible to him a few weeks ago was now truth—he trusted Whitney, trusted someone new in his life. It had been so long since Jack had been able to trust anything. He'd told her about growing up in Eagle's Ridge, about his best friends, and the things they used to do. How he'd gone into the Marines after college, wanting a greater purpose, wanting to serve in some way.

Whitney, in turn, told him about her "life of privilege," as she called it. She confessed she'd never had to work for anything, that everything had been handed to her. That this foray into a bakery was the first thing she'd done from start to finish on her own.

"That's not entirely true," he'd said. "You worked for a law degree."

"But only because I felt pressure to do it, not because I wanted to achieve something. I mean, I wanted to finish law school, but I knew from the beginning it wasn't what I wanted to do. That's why this is so important." She gestured to the apple pie she'd made for them. "This is the first time in my life that an idea and a goal are all mine. If I make it or if I don't, it's all on me. It's a really big deal to me."

"I get that," he'd said. He understood how hard it was to set goals and make them. Hell, he could scarcely go to the Coffee Corner with her that morning, but he'd done it, and he considered that an achievement.

He admired Whitney for not taking the easier way and the waiting job. He liked that she was focused on what sort of life she could make for herself, instead of letting life just happen to her. He could well imagine that a smart, beautiful woman like her would have had no trouble following a path to guaranteed success if she'd gone on to take the bar. She would have gone to work in her father's law firm, married well—probably the sort of guy who was a pillar of the community— and would have born the required number of children. She would never have had to worry about a thing. But

Whitney had obviously seen her life differently, and she seemed ready to fall on the sword to make it happen.

They also talked about movies and books, about sports—she was a fellow football fan—and dream vacations, in which beaches and mountains figured prominently for both of them. They talked about the current state of the world, of how such danger and beauty could co-exist. Much to Jack's surprise, they even talked about politics. These days, that didn't seem to be an easy conversation for anyone, but Jack and Whitney appeared to be on the same side on the issues.

Whitney's presence was a much-needed light in his life. The invisible weight of failure had been lifted; the curtains and windows had been opened and a ray of hope had filtered into his narrow world. He'd forgotten the tremendous healing power of the human touch, or how liberating it was to have someone to whom he could voice his thoughts. He was still filled with anxiety—not everything had changed—and yet, he could feel something opening up in him. The bricks were loosening and a few of them had fallen away. Sunlight streamed in through the cracks.

The other significant thing to happen over the weekend was that just after lunch on Saturday, when Whitney had gone out to look at some potential properties, Jack had called Sharon from the clinic. She'd answered on the first ring. From her tone, she sounded like a middle-aged, harried nurse and, even though she was speaking from home, she spoke furtively. She quickly acknowledged that the clinic had two sets of appointment books.

Terrence had told him as much, but Jack had

needed to hear it from her.

Sharon explained that the clinic had one set of appointment books that they kept on the computer, the schedule that made it seem as if Peter had been booked for a follow-up and hadn't showed for it.

"Why?" Jack had asked.

"There's not enough staff to handle all the people who need to come in," she said. "But if we turn them away, we don't get paid. So... they make it look like they came in, and then, we get paid."

"What happens to the money they collect? Did they try to hire more staff?"

"Nope," she'd said, sounding annoyed by it. "I don't know what they do with it. Anyway, that's why we have the manual schedule, and that's the true one. It's the one that shows how long some of these vets are having to wait to get help."

If what she was saying could be corroborated, Jack knew it was an explosive story. This sort of thing had supposedly been cleaned up with the new administration. "Sharon...I need a copy of that schedule."

"*No*," she'd said immediately. "*If I get caught, I'll be fired*," she'd whispered. "I'm a single mom, and I can't lose that job."

"I get it. I swear to you that I will never reveal my source. I'd go to jail first. I *swear* to you," he'd said, pressing his hand against his heart as if she could see him.

"You can swear all you want, but it's not the same thing for you. You have nothing to lose."

"That's not true," he'd said hoarsely as that cottony feeling in the back of his throat had returned, along with the thickness in his tongue, and he'd tried to swallow again. "I actually have a lot to lose."

"Yeah? Like what?"

"Peter died—"

"I know, and it was horrible," she'd said shortly. "But that's not you."

"But it is." He swallowed. "That's the thing, Sharon—it could very well be me."

His admission had been met with silence. He feared she thought he was feeding her a line to get what he wanted and get her fired.

"I have some of the, ah…" He'd tried to utter the words, tried to swallow against the cotton in his throat. "*Same issues*," he'd said in a rush.

Sharon had been silent, and Jack had panicked. He'd told her the truth and suddenly she wasn't speaking. For all he knew, she was making a note of his number, was going to trace it back to his apartment and report him to the—

"Okay," she said quietly. "Okay, okay. It will take me a few days. I'll call you when I have it."

Jack's heart was still racing, but he could swallow again. "Thank you, Sharon. For Peter, for me—*thank you*."

"I'll call you," she'd finally said, and had hung up.

———◆———

Whitney returned Saturday night, and that evening turned into Sunday morning, when Whitney and Jack stayed in bed and made love while it rained torrents outside. Midday, she said she had to bake.

"Then come back tonight," he'd said, surprisingly reluctant to let her go.

She'd peered closely at him, her gaze locked on his. "Am I imagining things? Or do you *like* me?"

He'd smiled. "You're okay," he'd said with a playful, noncommittal shrug.

"You *like* me like me," she'd said, poking him in the chest.

"Okay," he'd agreed, throwing his hands up. "I *like* you, like you."

Whitney had cast her radiant smile around him and Buster, and leaned in to kiss him. "Then I'll come back tonight." And then she'd practically skipped out of his apartment…because she liked him, too.

Christie called shortly after Whitney left. "What are you doing?" she'd asked.

"Hanging out." He made the mistake of chuckling when he said it. Christie homed in on that and dragged the truth out of him.

"The *dinner girl*," she said, her voice full of amazement. "She's pretty. And her cupcakes are to die for."

"Tell me," Jack agreed.

"No. *You* tell me," Christie insisted.

Jack told her that he had a friend. He didn't know what else to call it, other than amazing.

His "friend" returned that evening with a grocery bag. "Dinner Magic has nothing on me," she announced. Then hesitated. "Okay, maybe they do. But I can grill a chicken breast as well as anyone." She made a salad, roasted potatoes, and opened a bottle of wine she'd bought. She served the meal on his dining room table after stacking files and papers he stored there in an empty chair. It had been awhile since Jack had had a true sit-down meal.

While they dined, Whitney fretted about the

properties she'd seen, as none of them were perfect.

"What happened with Pioneer Square?" he asked, recalling her bit of monologue when they met for the first time.

"Pioneer Square," she said with a roll of her eyes, "is insanely expensive. And so small! I could have maybe squeezed in three bistro tables. But, Louisa and I are going out again later this week because she says she has found the perfect place…but between you and me, she says that every time." She punctuated that with a fork. "But she says this one is it. She says it's a little pricey, but checks all the boxes." She suddenly gasped. "You should come with me!"

The suggestion hit Jack square in the gut. He tried to smile, but his fear changed the vibe instantly. He then tried to laugh it off. "You don't want me hanging around—"

"Yes, I do! You know all about Seattle."

"Not really."

"Sure you do! You know more than me. Please?" she pleaded prettily. "We haven't been out of your apartment—"

"I know." He abruptly stood and walked into the kitchen. *Breathe in, breathe out. Think of puppies.* "It's just that I have this deadline—"

"Jack…I could really use your opinion. I need a grounded view."

He needed to *think*. He completed a circuit of the kitchen and walked back to the table and sat down. He pressed one fisted hand to his knee in a weak attempt to keep his breathing normal. "She's your friend. She'll give you a grounded view."

"She is my friend, but she also has a vested interest in getting me to agree to something," she said.

"You don't, and you're my friend, too."

Friends. He liked the sound of that. "We're friends, huh?" He reached for her hand across the table, twining his fingers with hers, his anxiety subdued for the moment.

"We're friends and *lovers,*" she said dramatically, and leaned across to him. "At least that's what I'm broadcasting to anyone who will listen. So far, that would be my sister and Louisa."

"And how do your friend and sister take the news of a lover?" He stroked her arm.

"With great interest," she said. "Louisa was mad she didn't know earlier. My sister was impressed at first, but when I told her that it had started Friday, she was no longer impressed. She said one weekend is not sufficient time for one to proclaim one has a lover."

"No?" He pulled Whitney toward him. Miraculously, his breathing had evened out. Funny how the chance of sex could do that to him. He should employ it more often. "What is the appropriate amount of time before you can declare you have taken a lover?"

She kissed him. "I don't know. What do you think? A week? Two weeks? Maybe it's based on the number of times you make love. How does three times sound?"

"It sounds, Miss Baldwin, as though you have taken a lover." He kissed her back.

The rest of the meal was forgotten. They ended up on the couch, a tangle of arms and legs and lips while the lights of Seattle glittered at them. And then they sat in their underwear and ate directly from the pie tin.

But Whitney left him later that night. "I have to

be up early tomorrow," she said when he complained about it. "I have an appointment with a tea room and a new Dinner Magic client. But I'll be back tomorrow with your meal delivery. And can I just say, I am *so happy* you ordered more things off the menu, Jack Carter."

"You ordered them, remember?"

"I know, but you didn't give me any grief. I have hope for you yet."

Jack had hope for him, too.

She dipped down to kiss Buster good-bye, too, and walked backward down the hall, wiggling her fingers at him, then turning to race to the elevator when it opened. She stuck her head out. "You're going with me to see this property Thursday, right? It's just around the corner from here." She waved, and the elevator door closed.

———◆———

Jack was smiling when he sat down for his Skype appointment with Dr. Pratt on Monday.

"Oh!" she said, with a look of surprise when she tuned in. "You look happy, Jack."

"I am," he said. "I had a great weekend." He gave her a quick, G-rated rundown of the weekend's events.

Dr. Pratt smiled. "So you trust her."

"Yeah." He smiled. He *did* trust her, and that was amazing to him.

"Well then! When are you going to take your girlfriend on a date?"

"She's not my girlfriend," he said.

"Let's say she is."

"Let's not."

"She won't be content cooking for you every day, you realize that, don't you? Women like to be treated like a princess from time to time. She's going to want to go out, and I think you should start to plan on how you will manage that. Where you might take her that feels safe."

Jack's heart leapt a little. He focused on a thread in the fraying hem of his jeans. "Actually, I think she's cool with things as they are. She knows I'm under a deadline." He tugged on the string. Maybe he ought to order a new pair.

"Are you going to tell her?" Dr. Pratt asked.

Jack tugged harder at the string. "Tell her what?"

"Jack."

He sighed. He looked up.

Dr. Pratt had cocked her head to one side. "Why do you think you don't want to tell her about your affliction?"

"Because it is an *affliction*," he said sharply, and then immediately shook his head. "Sorry. I don't know. Yeah, I do—I'm ashamed."

"Something awful happened to you, Jack. There is no shame in that. Your body and your mind are still processing that terrible thing, still coping—"

"It sounds stupid," he said curtly. It sounded weak. It sounded as if he couldn't handle himself, as though he wasn't a strong man, and the thing was, there was a time he could have handled himself and half of Seattle if he'd had to.

"I don't see it as stupid, and I think to say it is demeans everyone who struggles with a mental health disability. What I see is a legitimate physical and neurological response to trauma. And I would suggest that a remark like you just made adds to the stigmatization—"

"Doc," he said pleadingly. "I'm having a good time right now. I don't want to ruin it."

She smiled sadly, as though he were a disappointing child. "I would like for you to seriously consider why you believe that telling this woman the truth would ruin anything. Is she heartless?"

He snorted. "No."

"Do you think she has the capacity to understand that everyone comes to relationships with personal issues?"

"Yes," he said, "but this is different."

"Is it? I'm sure she has her own insecurities. And if she would judge you for what happened to you, then I wonder why she would be someone you wanted in your life."

It was a legitimate question, and his answer would be no, he wouldn't want her in his life. He needed someone who understood the beast that kept his throat in its jaws. But he did not want to take the chance that she wouldn't understand.

"Have you been to the coffee shop?" Dr. Pratt asked.

He perked up. "Three times," he said with a touch of pride. Granted, two times had been with Whitney, but still.

"That's good," she said. "So, you're feeling more comfortable with that environment?"

He hadn't thought of it that way, but yes, he was. "I guess, more or less."

"What would you think about trying something a little farther afield, such as the park?"

Jack physically recoiled at that absurd question.

"Are you serious? There are all kinds of people coming and going from that park. Remember, I can see it out my window," he said, pointing. "I mean, there's no way to know who those people are. The city doesn't control access. Anyone could walk in there. If you ask me, the city ought to—"

"Let's forget the park for now," she said quickly. "Is there something else on your street you could set as a goal?"

He thought about it a moment. "Whitney, she...she wants me to view a property with her. She's looking for a place to open a bakery. She says it's around the corner."

"That sounds like a great goal, Jack."

He was regretting it already. "It sounds like a terrible goal to me," he said. "What if...what if I lose my shit in front of her?" he asked in a near whisper. The very thought ratcheted up his panic, and he yanked so hard at the string in the hem of his jeans that he tore the denim.

"Let's talk about that. Whitney will be there, right?"

He nodded.

"Remember our conversation about having someone you trust nearby in case you have an attack?"

"But she doesn't know I get them," he irritably reminded her. "I don't *want* her to know."

"Chances are that if you practice the techniques we've talked about, you won't have one. I think it's worth a shot." She jotted it down on her notepad. "I think we should try it."

The "*we*" business annoyed him. Dr. Pratt could go anywhere she wanted, any time, with or without someone she trusted. "What if I have an attack?" he asked. "What then?"

"Then you will have a perfect opportunity to be honest with Whitney."

He clenched his jaw.

"Have you had any nightmares?" She looked down at her notes.

Amazingly, he had not. Thank God for small favors, because he couldn't imagine having one in front of Whitney. "Not since the last one I told you about."

"Are you taking your meds?"

He gave her a withering look.

"I'll take that as a no," she said pertly, and marked something on her file.

"You said this was fixable with cognitive therapy," Jack reminded her. "You said drugs were not necessary."

"I said drugs weren't necessary for the rest of your life. But you will no doubt remember that I also said you could ease your symptoms with some medicinal help. We just want to get your anxiety under control so you can learn the coping techniques."

This conversation was making him tense and irritable. "I'm making progress on my own." It was true—for the first time in a long time, he felt as if there was hope. Like maybe he really could beat this thing.

"I'm going to ask that you think about the things we've talked about today. Going a little farther than your safety circle, and perhaps being honest with Whitney about the challenges you face."

As it turned out, Jack did think about it. For days.

Twelve

"You might be a side chick, did you think of that?" Louisa asked as she and Whitney walked around the empty café that was available to rent.

This is what Whitney got for crowing about the new guy in her life. So, sue her already—the last real boyfriend she'd had was her first year of law school. After that ended, she hadn't had time for a true relationship. She was more than ready for one. And although it had only been a week, about the length of a *Bachelor* franchise show, Whitney felt good about things with Jack. She had the feeling this could go somewhere.

Until her friend said *that*, of course. Whitney looked at Louisa in her three-inch heels and short skirt, and her black hair slicked into a high ponytail and cascading down her back. Whitney couldn't begin to guess how much those hair extensions had set her back. "What do you mean?" Whitney demanded.

Louisa shrugged. "You know—someone on the side. Like, he's got a girlfriend and you're the side chick."

Whitney lifted her palms in the universal gesture of *what the hell?* "I'm telling you about a great guy I'm seeing, and *that's* your response?"

"Sorry," Louisa said, although she didn't sound sorry. "I'm just keeping it real. You invited him for drinks Tuesday, and he didn't come—"

"Because of his work," Whitney pointed out. It was true that Jack had bailed on her at the last minute. But then again, she'd asked him at the last minute, and he'd said *Sure*. She'd been sitting at the bar waiting for him when he'd texted and said, *So sorry, can't make it. Have to have this in by seven.* She'd given him the benefit of the doubt—maybe he didn't know that she was super punctual, and when she said she'd be waiting for him at six, she would be waiting for him at six.

"And he's already fifteen minutes late today," Louisa continued. "I don't think he's coming."

"He's coming," Whitney said, although she was wondering where the hell he was. Frankly, she had never realized how important punctuality was to her until this week and she was discovering it was *very* important. "And I'm not a side chick. I've been with him all week—when would he see his real girlfriend if I was a side chick?"

"Maybe she's on vacation," Louisa said. "Or at a conference. Maybe it's a long- distance relationship. I don't know. But you have to admit, it's weird that he hasn't taken you out. Or shown up for drinks. Or shown up today."

"It's not weird," Whitney said defensively.

"I mean, if I were you, I'd have to consider the possibility that he's spending all that time with you because you come and feed him."

"God, Louisa." Whitney was not liking this side of her friend. "Give him a minute, will you? And remember, we're still new at this—he hasn't had time to take me out, that's all."

"Okay." Louisa shrugged. "Let's look at the kitchen." She pointed to a door behind the counter.

Whitney tried to let Louisa's warning slide off her back as she looked around. What she'd had with Jack the last week felt really good. They had a lot in common. They had amazing physical chemistry. He was on a very heavy deadline, that was all.

But the minutes ticked by, and still no sign of Jack. She and Louisa looked at the kitchen, then at the bathrooms, the small office, the storage area, then returned to the storefront.

"Well?" Louisa stroked her long tail of hair. "What do you think?"

Whitney looked around her. This little café checked a lot of boxes. It was in a great location. The kitchen was big enough, had just the right amount of storage, and room out front for customers. "How much is the rent?"

"I think we could negotiate a rent of twenty-five grand a month," Louisa said.

Whitney's stomach flipped. "*Ouch*."

"Remember, we talked about your expectations," Louisa said. "You're not going to find a property in a location you want which checks all the boxes for less than that. I really think this is the one, Whit."

Whitney was a strong woman and a budding entrepreneur, but she really wished she had someone to help her make this decision. Someone who could talk through this thing with her. "But twenty-five—"

The door suddenly burst open and Jack surged through it as if he were being chased. He was breathing hard. He dragged his fingers through his hair, dropped Buster's leash, and then shoved his hands into his pockets. Buster jogged away, his nose to the floor.

Jack was perspiring so much that Whitney dug into her bag for a bottle of water. "Did you run here?" She handed him the bottle.

"What?" He shook his head to her offer of water. "Ah…yeah. No, I didn't run, I hurried. Sorry I'm late." He shifted a suspicious gaze to Louisa.

"This is Louisa Harris." Whitney moved to kiss him. His lips were cold, his body stiff. She eyed him, trying to figure out what was up with him. "I'm glad you made it."

"Me too," he said, sounding almost relieved.

Louisa stepped forward with a very silky smile. "So, you're *Jack*," she purred as she offered her hand.

Jack looked at her hand.

"I'm germ-free," Louisa said.

"No, that's…I know." He withdrew a hand and wiped it on his shirt before he offered it to shake Louisa's. "Hi," he said. "I'm sorry to barge in like this. It's nice to meet you, Louisa."

Louisa studied him a little too closely. "We were just finishing up. Would you like to have a look around? Or are you going to leave that to your dog?"

"Buster!" Jack called, and Buster trotted out of the men's restroom. Jack bent down and picked up his leash. "Let's have a look."

"I'll give him a tour." Whitney took the leash

from his hand and handed it to Louisa. "You'll like Buster."

Louisa looked down at the soulful brown eyes and squatted down. "I *will*," she said.

Whitney linked her arm through Jack's and pulled him away from Louisa and into the kitchen. Once they were out of Louisa's earshot, she said, "What's wrong?"

"Wrong? Nothing. Sorry I'm late." He shoved his hands in his pockets again. He kept his gaze on the floor.

He seemed...*verklempt*. It was the first word that popped into Whitney's mind. Something *was* wrong—he was nervous and distracted. She touched his face. "Jack?"

He flinched at first, but then caught her hand and held it tightly. *Too* tightly. "I'm really sorry, Whitney. I got caught up."

"You didn't answer my text."

"My phone died." He turned away from her to view the kitchen, but did not let go of her hand. His felt so strangely clammy.

He swallowed hard. "What do you think?"

"I think it's perfect," she said. "There's a lot of foot traffic down this street, which is great."

"Right." He fixed his gaze on the stove.

"And it has an extra oven," she said. "Only one baker's rack, so I'll have to get a second one."

Jack was not listening. His jaw was clenched, and now he had his eye on the door between the kitchen and the front counter.

"Do you want to know how much?" she asked.

Jack suddenly looked at her. He was still perspiring. "For...?"

"This place. The rent is twenty-five thousand dollars a month to rent."

He stared at her. "Twenty-five *thousand*? That's a lot of money."

Whitney snorted. "Tell me about it. If you didn't run here, why are you sweating?"

Her blurted question startled him. "Am I?" He let go of her hand, swiped at his temple and looked at his fingers.

"So?" Louisa called, stepping into the kitchen with Buster. "What do you think, Jack? Don't you think it's perfect for your girl?"

"Ah...looks good," Jack agreed.

"I'm trying to convince her to let me work my magic and see what sort of deal I can make her." Louisa handed the leash end to Jack. "She won't find a better location for this price in Seattle, don't you agree?"

"I don't know." He looked at Whitney. "It's a *lot* of money."

"You have to pay to play," Louisa said. "Right, Whit?"

Whitney nodded, but her stomach was a mess. Her nerves were suddenly and unusually frayed—with the amount of money it would take to set this place up and then rent it. With Jack and the strange way he was acting.

"In the meantime, Jack, you should take Whitney out for dinner to celebrate," Louisa chirped.

Whitney coughed down a gasp. She didn't want to look at Jack, but of course she did, and he sort of smiled at her with his hands jammed into his pockets and the sheen of perspiration still on his face.

"Okay, you two." Louisa looked at her watch.

"I've got another appointment."

The three of them and Buster went out onto the street. Louisa locked things up while Jack stood with his back pressed against the window of the empty café, Buster beside him.

With her gaze on her phone, Louisa said, "I need to run." She looked up at Jack. "Are we going to lure you out for those drinks soon? I would love to chat." She patted his arm. "Don't look so skeptical—I'm a lot of fun with a cocktail."

"Sure," he said tightly.

"Great! Toodle-oo for now," Louisa said, and with a wave, she strode down the street to catch a cab.

Whitney folded her arms and looked at Jack. "Seriously, are you all right?" she asked. "You're acting weird."

"I'm fine," he said, but he looked at Buster.

"You can hardly look at me, and you looked at Louisa like she was crazy when she asked if she could buy you a drink."

"You're right." He reached for her waist, drawing her into his side, up against the door of the bakery, and held her tight. "I apologize, Whitney. I've got a lot on my mind." He kissed her temple.

"You and me both," she muttered, and leaned into him. "Do you want to buy me a drink?"

"I've got a better idea. I'll make you one. There's a bodega on my street. We can pop in there and pick up a few things, and I'll make you a cocktail that will knock your socks off."

Something niggled in the back of Whitney's head. That niggle, which sounded an awful lot like Louisa, reminded her that in the week they'd spent together, Jack had never offered to take her anywhere.

Side chick.

Jack grabbed her hand. "You ready?"

"You know what?" She squeezed his hand. "If it's okay with you, I'm going to take a rain check."

"A rain check?" He looked at her with confusion. "Why? Is it because I was so late? I am so sorry, Whitney, but I—"

"No, it's not that," she assured him, although it was definitely that. She didn't understand why he was so edgy, so jumpy. "I'm just not all here." She gestured to her head. "I need to run some numbers, and I don't think I'd be good company."

She could tell by his expression that he wasn't buying it. He touched her face and stroked back of bit of her hair. "Are you sure?"

"I'm sure."

He frowned as he leaned down to kiss her temple. "Okay," he said reluctantly. He kissed her cheek, his lips lingering for a moment. Warmth began to spiral through Whitney. "But if you need to talk, you know where to find me," he murmured, and kissed her lips.

Yes, she knew exactly where to find him—in his apartment. Whitney wrapped her arms around his neck and kissed him back. She kissed him in a way she hoped would show that she was into him, *really* into him, and needed for him to be into her, too. He was hard-bodied, his lips soft, and when he wrapped his arm around her waist, he held her too tightly, as if he were afraid she would float away. There was something quietly desperate in the way he held her.

"I'll see you tomorrow?"

"Of course you will." She managed a smile.

He kissed her once more, then looked down at Buster. "Let's go." Buster hopped to his feet, his body pointing in the direction of home, his tail wagging.

Jack moved as if he meant to walk away, but he suddenly turned back and cupped her face. "Don't worry, Whitney," he said. "Please don't worry."

"About...?"

"About...about anything," he said uncertainly. "If you let it, it will consume you."

She must have looked confused because he said, "I'm only trying to say that if you let worry take over, it can lead you to do things you don't normally do."

His earnestness was odd. Did she seem so worried? "Okay..." she said carefully. "Thanks for your concern."

Jack pressed his lips together. He gave her a short nod, then turned, and with his head down, he began to walk quickly, his limp noticeable, and Buster trotting alongside him.

Whitney's phone rang. She dug in her bag for it, and when she had it, she looked up, intending to wave one last time, but Jack had already disappeared.

"Hello?"

"Hello, Whitney, how are you?"

Whitney closed her eyes and wished that a massive cell phone tower hack would happen right now. This day was quickly deteriorating. "Hi, Dad."

"At last, I get you on the phone," he said.

Whitney winced at the number of times she'd let his call roll to voice mail. "Yep! I've just been really busy."

"How are things going with your project?" her father asked.

Her project. As if she were in middle school and wrapping up her construction of a model of the solar system. "It's going *great*." She walked down the street toward the bus stop. "In fact, I'm kind of in the middle of something."

"What's that?" he asked.

"Well, I just looked at a café," she said. "My realtor found the perfect place." Yeah, that was it—strike before he had the opportunity.

"She did, huh?" her father said. "Well, maybe I can have a look when I'm in Seattle in a few weeks."

Her sister *had* warned her. "So, you're coming to Seattle!" she said brightly.

"I am. I would like to see how you're doing and what you've accomplished since your move there."

"Dad—"

"I'm not coming to judge you, Whitney," he said with a tinge of exasperation. "I *care* about you. I'm *interested.* You're my daughter, and I want to know what you're doing, how things are progressing."

That was a lovely thing to say, but there had been an ocean of hard words between them, so Whitney was more than a little skeptical. She turned in to a convenience store and started down the aisle. "Okay, well...great," she said with as much cheer as she could muster. "I'll bake a cake." She laughed.

Her father didn't. "I'm looking forward to seeing you, Whitney."

She stopped in the middle of the aisle and stared at a display of deodorants. "Me too, Dad," she said with more enthusiasm than she felt. She hated this about their relationship. She loved her father; she really did love him. But they were very different people, with very different views of the world, and she thought it was healthier for them both if they lived in different cities.

"I'll call you with my plans," her father said. "So

please pick up when I call."

"I will," she said weakly.

"And call your mother," he added. "She worries about you."

Whitney glanced heavenward. "Okay, all right," she promised. "Talk to you later?"

"I love you, Whitney." He hung up.

A man passed in front of Whitney, and she stepped back, still staring at the display of deodorants. Her parents loved her, she had no question of that. She only wished they could be more supportive of what she wanted from life.

But what if they were right? What if this idea she had was as bad as they seemed to think? She thought about how much the rent would cost for that little café, how many cupcakes she'd have to sell every month. She thought about her inheritance which, while a sizable amount, could only carry her for a few months if she couldn't cut it. She thought about the advertising and marketing, and having to hire people to help her run it. It was easy to imagine these things, but they all felt almost impossible to do.

It was sort of the same with Jack. It was easy to imagine that he was the perfect guy for her, but in reality, there was something a little off that was bothering her. Something didn't make sense.

The thought occurred to her that maybe she was trying to fit round pegs into square holes all around her life. Maybe it was time to figure out what the round pegs were.

She turned toward the front of the store, wondering why she'd ever come in here, and walked outside, her thoughts as gloomy as the weather.

Thirteen

Jack had been inexcusably late to meet Whitney because he could not make himself leave his apartment. In spite of the techniques Dr. Pratt had taught him, his fear had begun to choke him when he thought about rounding the street corner at the light. It was simply a matter of not being able to see—or imagine—what was around the corner.

It was that kind of nonsensical thinking that made his condition so insidious—he *knew* the thoughts popping into his head were utter bullshit, and yet, his body wouldn't believe him. His body didn't trust him at all.

But Jack was determined to go for Whitney, and in the end, it had taken a mad dash for the open elevator with Buster at his side. He told himself if he didn't make it, he wasn't going. But if the doors stayed open...

By the time he made it to the café, they were

finishing up, and Whitney was not happy, clearly, and had sent him home. So basically, what should have been a victory was really more of a disaster.

He was going to have to hand in his man card if he kept this up.

By the time he reached his apartment at a near sprint, he was convinced he'd blown it. He was obsessed with the idea that he had ruined the best thing that had happened to him in two years because he didn't know how to do this anymore, couldn't get past himself to be a decent boyfriend.

Frank was still behind the desk when Jack banged through the glass doors of his building with Buster in tow. "Back so soon, boss?" Frank asked jovially. He was probably wondering why Jack had chosen this day, of all days, to venture past the front door.

Good question, Frank.

"Ah…yeah. Just had a quick errand." He flashed Frank a smile as he beelined for the elevator. He punched the button a few times in futility, fearful that he might actually have to talk to Frank and reveal what a pansy he was. But the elevator arrived quickly, and he and Buster were on it in a flash.

Once inside his apartment, Jack collapsed onto the couch, inexplicably exhausted. Buster crawled up onto the couch and stretched himself across Jack's lap.

Even Buster thought he'd ruined everything.

Jack sighed. "Sorry, buddy." He stroked his dog. Buster's calming influence began to settle over him like a veil. He thought about the beta-blockers in his medicine cabinet. Maybe he needed to do it. It had gotten too easy to stay in, to have life delivered to him in an array of bags and boxes because America was such a great country.

Still, beta-blockers worried him. *Look what happened to Peter! That could be him. He could become suicidal if he wasn't careful.*

But in the next moment, Jack was berating himself. He wasn't Peter. He was imagining things now. It was almost as if the door to a vast array of anxiety disorders had been opened in Afghanistan.

He leaned his head back and closed his eyes, trying not to think too much. Just as he was dozing off, his phone rang. Jack lurched awake; Buster hopped down. He dug frantically in his pocket for his phone, certain it was Whitney. "Hello, Whitney?"

"Sharon."

"Oh," he said. "Hi, Sharon." He stood and started to pace.

"Hi. I have the, ah…the thing," she said.

"You do? Can you get it to me?"

She grunted at that. "You can pick it up. I've done what I said I would do."

"Okay." Jack didn't know how in the hell he would do that, but he'd figure something out. "At your office?"

"Are you crazy? No, at the library downtown. The big one. You know what I'm talking about?"

Jack winced. "I do."

"I'll be there tomorrow at two, on my lunch break. I'll be outside the main entrance."

"Okay," he said. "Thanks so much, Sharon."

"Yeah." She clicked off.

Jack put down his phone and dragged his fingers through his hair. His phone rang again, and he picked it up absently, his thoughts racing around how he could possibly meet Sharon at the library. A public place where people streamed in and out all day. "Jack Carter," he said.

"Jack."

Noah. A smile instantly spread across Jack's face. "Noah! Hey buddy, how the hell are you?"

"Okay," he said, but then he made a strange sound. "Actually, not so good. Listen, I can't talk long, but I thought you'd want to know that Lainey passed away yesterday."

Jack's heart broke away from its moorings and fell to his toes. He knew she was sick—he even knew it was terminal—but still. *So soon?* "Oh God," he whispered, and sank down onto his couch. "My God. Noah...I am so sorry. Was she...was there pain?"

"I don't think so," Noah said. "She was heavily medicated." He paused, and Jack could hear his labored breathing. "It sucks, man." His voice cracked.

"Yeah, it sucks," Jack agreed. He thought of that sweet girl with the long brown hair and clear brown eyes. Lainey hadn't been his first love, but she'd definitely been a big love. More important, she'd been his friend. A *real* friend. She kept up a correspondence with him while he was in the Marines, even though she was working full-time and had a family of her own. She'd always had time for him and Noah. Lainey hadn't known about his anxiety disorder, but if she had, Jack was certain she would have been on the phone with him as often as Dr. Pratt.

"Look, I can't be at her funeral, but it's set for Sunday."

"Okay," Jack said slowly.

"You can look it up online, the time and details," Noah said. "I've got it written down here somewhere, but..."

"I'll look it up."

"It would mean a lot to me if you could go, Jack," Noah said. "One of us ought to be there to say good-bye."

"Sure." Jack's pulse surged. "Yeah, I...thanks for letting me know. Are you all right?"

"Me?" Noah sighed wearily. "I'm relieved, I think. It's been hard on her."

"I can't imagine," Jack muttered.

"Are *you* all right?" Noah asked. "Dude, no one has seen you."

"No, I'm good. Just busy. Really busy," Jack said.

"Yeah," Noah said absently. "Okay, well...I've got some calls to make."

"Take care, buddy."

"You do the same." Noah hung up.

Tears burned in the back of Jack's eyes. It was hard to believe Lainey was really gone. He was going to make it to the funeral. He was going to be there for Lainey and Noah, and he wasn't going to let this goddam disease or condition or whatever it was stop him.

———◆———

Jack didn't know how long he'd been sitting on his couch with his head between his hands, but when his buzzer sounded, but he was surprised that the light of day was fading. He dragged himself to the intercom. "Yeah, Frank?"

"Tristan," came the response. "Wanted to let you know that Ms. Baldwin is on her way up."

Whitney was here? "Thanks." Jack wiped his face

with his sleeve and quickly combed his hair with his fingers.

He opened the front door, and Buster put himself at the threshold. The elevator dinged, and his tail began to wag furiously. Jack tried to pull himself together as Whitney walked down the hall toward him.

"I'm sorry I came over without warning," she said.

He was very glad that she had.

"My dad called. I went home, but I started thinking that maybe I..." She paused and peered at him. "What's wrong?" She reached him, her blue eyes filled with concern. "Are you okay?"

He wasn't okay. He felt himself quaking. "I got some bad news," he said, his voice shaking too. "I lost a good friend."

"Oh no," she said. "Jack, I'm so *sorry*."

She wrapped her arms around him and Jack sank into her, his arms wrapping around her waist. He bent his head and pressed his face into her neck. He needed her touch, her warmth. How had he allowed himself to isolate himself from so many people and so much of his life?

"Come on." She took his hand in hers. "Tell me about it." She led him to the couch, made him sit.

Jack told her a little about Lainey when they'd looked at the picture he had of him and the guys. Tonight, he spoke of her haltingly at first, as every word was a sharp reminder she was gone. How he'd always known her through one of his best friends, her cousin Noah. How when they'd entered high school, she was no longer the skinny girl who used to follow them around, but a beautiful, sweet, caring girl.

"Ah, Jack…this must be so hard for you."

He gave her a rueful half smile. "Thanks, Whitney. It means a lot to me that you're here."

She suddenly kicked off her shoes and crawled onto his lap, straddling him. Her skirt flared out around them, and he could feel the flesh of her thighs against his jeans. "I'm *really* sorry," she murmured, and kissed his face, the bridge of his nose.

Jack's feelings began to flow away from grief and into desire. His hands found her hips. He was hard, his sorrow mutating into need for a woman's touch, for comfort. He slipped his hand into her panties, into her damp warmth, and began to stroke her. Whitney was still kissing him, moving on him, panting into his ear. Jack stood with her, holding her legs wrapped around his waist, and walked her down the hall into his bedroom.

Whitney was so beautiful to him. His hunger for her smothered the memory of all that had happened today, his disappointment at not being the man Whitney desired, or the boy Lainey had wanted. He craved nothing but the sensation of being with Whitney, of feeling a woman's skin next to his, beneath his lips and fingers. He needed nothing more than to rock along on a wave of pleasure, until she fell apart beneath him and there was nothing left of him. He wanted to sink into that place where there was no anxiety, no fear—just this moment, this passionate, exhilarating, intimate moment.

When they were spent, they talked until the early morning hours about their first loves and lost loves. Jack didn't know exactly when they drifted off, but he woke up early the next morning with her hair in the corner of his mouth and her leg draped across his. He turned his head, toward the window.

The top of Buster's head and his eyes were the only thing visible at the edge of his bed, but Jack could hear the sound of his tail against the carpet. "I got you, buddy," Jack muttered sleepily, and scratched Buster's ears before he disentangled himself from Whitney.

He was preparing Buster's breakfast when Whitney appeared, her hair sexily disheveled around her face, the imprint of the quilt on his bed pressed into one cheek. She pushed her hair back, then looked at the clock. "Oh my God!" she suddenly exclaimed. "What am I doing? I have an appointment with a bistro on University and Seventh! I need to go home and bake some cupcakes!" She whirled around and ran for his bedroom.

Jack followed her. He leaned his shoulder against the doorframe and watched her feverishly gather her things. "You'll come tonight?"

"I will," she said as she pulled on her skirt.

"Hey," Jack said, and ignored the tiny swell of nausea in his belly. "Do me a favor?"

"Of course!" she said, but she wasn't looking at him. She was searching through her bag for something.

"Would you mind picking up something for me?"

She laughed. She tied her hair into a knot at her nape. "Is it for me? What is it? Tickets to a play? Flowers? No, wait…new muffin tins."

Jack smiled. "A woman who has some papers for me. I need them for this deadline, but I can't get out today. I've got to see about getting to Eagle's Ridge for Lainey's funeral this weekend."

"Oh." Her bright smile faded a little. "Papers, you

said?"

"She's, ah…she's supposed to meet me at the central library at two."

"The library?"

"It's kind of complicated. But the library is near University and Seventh," he said. It was a few blocks, not terribly out of Whitney's way. "I can text her and tell her you're going to swing by. That is, if you wouldn't mind. She'll be waiting outside the main doors."

Whitney's expression was oddly dubious. "Ah…sure, I guess."

His relief was so great, he laughed. "Thanks, Whitney." He wrapped his arms around her, hugging her close.

"I mean…it's going to take you all day to arrange getting to Eagle's Ridge?" she said into his chest.

Jack tried to laugh that off, but it came out like a garbled cough. "It's just work, you know, and…the arrangements."

"Sure," she said, but her voice sounded a little curt. She pushed out of his embrace to pick up her things. "I really have to get out of here. So, I'm meeting this lady at the library."

Jack told her where to meet Sharon and then watched her leave in a flurry of shoes and bags and hurried kisses.

She wasn't crazy about this favor, he could tell.

But he had another, bigger problem. Jack sighed and went back to his office. He sat at his computer and held his head in his hands a few minutes, worrying about how he would ever make it to Eagle's Ridge.

Fourteen

———◆———

Whitney arrived at the library, pulling her rolling cooler behind her. The woman was exactly where Jack said she would be—leaning up against the wall just outside the main doors. She looked a little older than Jack had said, but she wore nurse's scrubs and had a black tote bag over one shoulder.

"Hi," Whitney said as she reined her cooler to a halt. "Are you Sharon?"

The woman started. She eyed Whitney, and then the cooler. "What is *that*?"

Whitney looked down. "A cooler," she said.

"For *what?*"

"For food," Whitney said, confused. She bent over and opened the top of it, removed a cupcake from a box on top, and held it out to the lady. "Would you like one?"

Sharon stared at the cupcake that looked like the Cookie Monster eating a small chocolate chip cookie.

They were delightful, if Whitney thought so herself. "I'm a baker," she said, probably unnecessarily, because surely only bakers wheeled cupcakes around. "I make these. It's chocolate—do you like chocolate? I'm always amazed at the number of people who *don't* like chocolate. Me, I eat it every day. You probably guessed that." She gave a short bark of laughter then silently reprimanded herself for filling all the available air around them with chatter.

Apparently, Whitney would never know if this woman—Sharon, Jack had said—liked chocolate or not, because she withdrew a padded mailing envelope from her tote bag and thrust it at Whitney. "Here." She turned away, striding off down the sidewalk as though the library were on fire.

Whitney stared after her, her mouth agape. "Thanks a *lot*." She returned the masterful Cookie Monster cupcake to its box. She tossed the envelope into her tote and went on to meet with the manager at the bistro.

A few hours later, Whitney made it to Jack's place with the ingredients for the cauliflower tetrazzini she'd made him order. She was not on top of her game—she was feeling nauseated from having eaten two Cookie Monsters in the space of two minutes in a momentary lapse into self-pity after her meeting at the bistro.

"Hey." Jack greeted her at the door of his apartment. "What's wrong?"

"Miserable day." She accepted his embrace, pressing her forehead against his chest.

"Why?"

"Oh, nothing. I just visited with the cutest bistro in all of Seattle, and they loved my Cookie Monster cupcakes and the teacakes I made this morning—for the first time, mind you—but of course it all hinges on that stupid health department certificate," she said. "I never thought finding a bakery location would be *this* hard." She moved to pass him, but Jack caught her hand. "Maybe I should stop lining up work. I just assumed I'd be up and running by now, you know? Why are you holding my hand?"

"Wait here." He disappeared into the living room while Whitney and Buster stood foot to paw. "Okay, come in," he said.

Whitney walked into the living room and gasped with delight. There were flowers on every conceivable surface—the kitchen bar, the coffee table, the bookshelves—and the table had been set with real china and candles. "What is *this?*" A smile lit her face.

Jack took her by the hand, pulled her around to the couch and sat her down. "Cheer up." He pulled off one of her boots and began to rub her foot. "You found the perfect place, remember? You'll be up and running in no time."

"I know, I know. But the perfect place costs a small fortune." She sighed, leaned her head against the couch and closed her eyes as he worked on her foot. "Jack, that's, like, *orgasmic.*"

He chuckled and continued working on her foot for a few minutes. When he moved to the next one, she pulled the mailer out of her bag. "Here's your package," she said. "I don't know how I feel about your friend. She flat-out rejected my offer of a Cookie Monster cupcake."

"She did?"

"Actually, she never answered. She just looked at

the cupcake like it was poison and I was a lunatic. She was even miffed that I had a rolling cooler. What's up with her?"

"Ah, well," Jack said, his focus on her foot, "she's a source. Sources can be suspicious. I promised I wouldn't say anything about her."

"Not even to me?" Whitney teased him, nudging him with her foot.

"Even to you," he said. "She'd get in a lot of trouble if anyone knew she was talking to me."

"Well, now you have my undivided attention. This sounds like espionage. You're not a spy, are you?" She suddenly laughed. "Are you a *spy*, Jack? Please tell me you're a spy."

"Not a spy." Jack let go of her foot. He moved to sit beside her on the couch and put his arm around her shoulders. "I told you one of the articles I'm working on is about a VA clinic. It gets money from the VA to help vets."

"So why the espionage?" she asked curiously.

He considered the question a moment. "I had a friend—Peter was his name—and he had some major issues after his tour in Afghanistan. He had trouble getting into the Victory clinic at first, but he finally did. They put him on some meds. Well, the meds weren't working, and they were making him feel worse. So, Peter tried to go back, but he couldn't get an appointment. That's really strange, because once the clinic knew he was having psychotic side effects, they should have gotten him in straightaway. But Peter was waitlisted, and before they got him in, he died."

"Oh my God," Whitney said. "What happened?"

"He killed himself," Jack said.

She gasped. "No!"

"Afraid so," he said. "But the clinic denied he was waitlisted and said he missed his appointments. I've been nosing around about that, and I got Sharon, who works at the clinic, to admit there are two schedules. They have a schedule they show the VA in order to receive their money, and they have the real one. The waitlist. Sharon didn't want to do it, but she made a copy of the real one, and that's what's in the package."

"*Oh,*" Whitney said.

"Hopefully whatever she sent will help me open this story up."

Whitney was silent a few moments, thinking about that. "Did you make the arrangements to go to Eagle's Ridge?"

"I did." He'd been so relaxed, but he suddenly sat up, bracing his arms on his knees.

"What's the plan?"

"I'm renting a car." He rubbed his hands on his knees. "Going early Sunday, back in the evening."

He kept rubbing his hands on his knees, which Whitney took as a sign he was very torn up about Lainey's death. Two friends lost—how hard that must have been for Jack.

"Do you want me to keep Buster?" she asked.

He turned his head to look at her. "Where...at your place?"

"Sure, why not? Buster could use a change of scenery, couldn't you, Buster?" she asked. Hearing his name, Buster appeared to stick his nose under her hand. He looked at her so adoringly that Whitney's heart melted a little.

"You don't mind?"

"Not at all," she said. "I could use a little company."

"That's…that's really nice of you." His gaze filled with an expression of affection that surprised Whitney. No one had looked at her like that in a very long time—with appreciation. It made her feel warm and sparkly inside, and she reached for his hand, squeezed his fingers. "Let's go somewhere," she said. "Get a drink, have some dinner, take our mind off everything."

"I would love to do that." He said it so earnestly that Whitney was about to stand up, shove the ingredients of his meal kit into the fridge, and grab her bag.

"But I can't." He winced. "I've got too much to do to get ready."

Whitney's doubts and emotions crashed into each other. She tried to formulate a response, perhaps one that pointed out how he was only going to Eagle's Ridge for a day, and there couldn't be that much to do to "get ready." Or maybe even point out how he never left his apartment, and when he did, he couldn't wait to get back to it.

"And I had planned to cook tonight and serve *you*," he added, and suddenly smiled, casting his arms around him at all the flowers. "I made it as romantic as I could."

Whitney looked at the flowers and the candles. He *had* gone to some trouble. "I see what you did there," she said lightly. But she still felt a little funky about it. She couldn't quite put her finger on why, because he *was* making a romantic gesture. But once again, something seemed off.

He seemed to sense her hesitation because he

suddenly grabbed her up in his arms and kissed her, his hand cupping her jaw, his lips nipping at hers. "Thank you for understanding," he murmured.

Whitney didn't understand him at all. She couldn't help wonder, as she kissed him back and felt herself turning to warm, gooey molasses, whether she had landed in a relationship that *felt* so damn right but was practically all wrong for her.

Was that even possible?

Was she overthinking it?

She tried to shake that feeling off as she sat at the bar to watch Jack make dinner, drinking the wine he poured her and eating the olives he'd ordered, while giggling at how inept he was in the kitchen. Gradually, her misgivings began to melt away. How could she possibly think anything was wrong when she was being wined and dined by a guy as hot and sexy as Jack?

After dinner, they played a silly board game that had them both collapsing into giggles. Whitney refused to dwell on the fact that he'd said he had too much to do to go out, and yet, had the time to play a game. And that night, when they made love, she didn't think about anything other than how wonderful it felt to be with him, to feel him inside her. She thought only of how magical and perfect it all was and had all the fairy-tale feels a girl was supposed to have when she was falling in love.

God, was she falling in *love* with him?

Maybe. It sort of felt that way.

In spite of the weird vibe she got from him at times, and the questions she had about what was really going on in that beautiful head of his, something about Jack just clicked with her.

———————◆———————

The next morning, Whitney kissed Jack good-bye for the weekend. They'd mutually decided she'd come back Monday with Buster when she brought his Dinner Magic meal kit.

She and Buster trundled home to her little studio apartment, taking time to walk through a park and by a pet store, where Buster was quite excited to have a look at the kittens in a crate high above him. She bought him a toy and some treats to chew on while she worked.

Later that night, when Whitney crawled into her bed—just two mattresses stacked one on top of the other—Buster decided he liked that option better than the floor and climbed up next to her. The next morning, the loud snoring of a dog curled up beside her awakened her.

She and Buster read the morning paper, walked down to get a coffee and some eggs, then returned to her studio. She busied herself with chores, and Buster followed her around the two hundred and fifty square feet she was allotted.

Midday, she decided she wanted to make a rhubarb pie and decorate it with an array of edible flowers. But as she made a list of ingredients she would need, she realized that her deep-dish pie tin was at Jack's. "Great," she muttered and glanced at her charge. "We need a walk, don't we, pup? We'll go get some fresh rhubarb from Pike's Place, then run by Jack's and get the pie tin."

Buster wagged his tail with enthusiasm.

It was a beautiful day, with a gorgeous blue sky overhead. The only thing that would have made their midday Sunday jaunt more exciting was if Jack had been with them. Whitney could imagine them going to Pike's Place, then strolling through the park, then getting some ice cream. A picture-perfect Sunday afternoon, just like the movies had taught her to want.

In the lobby of Jack's apartment building, Frank was sitting behind the desk.

"You work weekends, too?" Whitney asked.

"Nah." He rubbed an eye. "The new kid called in sick. I just got here."

"I'm going to run up and get a pie tin," she said.

"Sure," Frank said. "I'll call and let him know you're on the way."

"Don't bother, he's not there." She held out his apartment keys and jangled them in front of Frank.

"We're making progress," Frank said approvingly, and waggled his brows at her.

"We *are*," she agreed, and with a laugh, she and Buster headed for the bank of elevators.

At the door of Jack's apartment, Whitney stuck the key in the lock and turned. But it was unlocked. "He forgot to lock it," she muttered. She opened the door, and Buster suddenly broke from her side, racing down the hall with the leash trailing behind him, then turning in to the hall that led to the bedrooms.

"He's not here!" she called after the dog. She put down her bag and shut the door, then walked down the hall after the dog. But as she neared the last room at the end of the hall, something unpleasant curled in her belly. She had the creepy feeling that someone *was* in there. "Buster!" she hissed, and slowly, carefully, inched toward the door.

Someone was in there, all right. It was Jack, sitting in the corner of his room, his knees drawn up to his chest. He looked ashen, and her first instinct was that he was sick. "Oh my God, Jack." She ran across the room to him, falling to her knees beside him and pushing Buster out of the way. "What happened? Are you okay?" She put her hand to his forehead. It was damp and warm.

"I'm fine," he said, his voice gravelly. He tried to push her hand away, but he misjudged where she was. He was sweating profusely, his shirt soaked through, and his breathing seemed ragged.

"I'm calling 911." She moved to stand.

"*No!*" he said sharply, and caught her arm, this time with surprising strength. "Don't call anyone," he said through gritted teeth. "I'm *fine*."

Alarmed, Whitney jerked her arm free. "No, you're not. You're sweating, and your breathing is shallow, and you look like hell."

"Just...just give me a minute." He pulled Buster onto his lap, cradling the dog.

Whitney sank back on her heels, trying to make sense of it. "What is happening right now?" she asked him. "What is going on?"

"Nothing." He buried his face in Buster's neck.

"It's not *nothing,* Jack. It is definitely something. You're supposed to be at a funeral and you look like you're dying or—*Jesus,* is it drugs?"

"Drugs!" he said, sounding annoyed. "Of course, it's not *drugs.*" He pushed Buster off his lap and came to his feet, using the wall as leverage. He moved past her and stumbled into the bathroom. He opened a medicine cabinet so roughly that several amber pill bottles tumbled out.

Whitney had goose bumps, felt as if she were seeing someone else in Jack's skin. "What is all that?

You're not okay—"

"Just let it go, Whitney!" he shouted.

Whitney was so taken aback by his tone and the murderously angry look on his face that she took a step backward. "Okay." She held up both hands. And then she walked out of his room quickly, propelled by a lethal mix of anger and fear. She felt stupid; she felt used. She grabbed up her bag, had a thought, and raced into the kitchen to get her pie tin. When she had it in hand, she whirled toward the door, but Jack stood there, blocking her way, and her heart climbed to her throat.

"I'm sorry," he said.

"I need to go."

"Don't—"

"I have to get out of here!" She pushed past him.

Jack grabbed her arm again. "Please let me explain—"

"Let *go* of me!" she shrieked, and Jack instantly dropped his hand.

Whitney didn't want to listen to him—all her doubts, all the times she'd felt something was off, was part of a nauseating mix of fear and betrayal and white-hot anger. *How could she have been so stupid?*

"*Whitney!*" he called after her, his voice full of torment.

Whitney paused at the door. She closed her eyes and took a deep breath. She opened the door, and slowly turned back to him. He stood in the hallway, drenched with sweat, a terrified expression. "Look, Jack," she said. "I really like you. I do. But I don't know what's going on with you, and it scares me. This is just too weird for me."

"I know." He reached a hand toward her, as if

trying to hold her in place as he took an uneasy step forward. "Believe me, I know how weird it is."

"If you know, then why don't you…" She made a frantic motion with her hand. "*Do* something!"

"I'm trying."

"You're not trying hard enough," she said, and bolted through the door. If he called her, she didn't hear him. She didn't care whether he did. She'd gotten too emotionally invested, and the warning signs had been there all along.

She reached the elevator and punched the down button hard enough to hurt her finger. The door instantly slid open. Whitney stepped back without looking at the person stepping off the elevator. Her mind was too far from here, racing toward all the things she wanted to hate herself for in this moment.

"Hey! Whitney, it's me, Christie."

Whitney jerked her gaze up to Jack's sister. She was smiling.

"How are you? Oh hey, your cupcakes were *dope*," she said. "I can't believe you don't have shops all over downtown—"

"Thanks." Whitney tried to step around Christie before the elevator doors closed. Unfortunately, she couldn't reach them in time, and no hammering on the button was going to bring the car back.

Christie glanced down the hall, to Jack's open door, then to Whitney. "What's wrong?"

"Nothing."

"Did something happen?"

"No. Sort of." Whitney tried to avoid Christie's gaze, but Christie kept moving and putting herself in front of Whitney.

"Sort of like what?"

"I'm sorry," Whitney said. "I don't want to rag on your brother, I don't. But he's got some issues."

"He sure does," Christie readily agreed. "Did he tell you?"

She had Whitney's undivided attention. "Tell me what?"

Christie's face darkened. She took Whitney's hand. "Come on," she said sternly. "He's going to tell you, or I'm going to kick his stupid ass."

Fifteen

Jack was still in the same spot he was when Whitney walked out, still reeling from the realization that when she left, she took the best thing to have happened to him since Afghanistan. He didn't feel the ravage of anxiety—he felt numb. Everything else that had happened today was a distant dream.

He'd screwed up.

Jack wasn't surprised to see Christie when the door opened—after all, he'd called her from the airport where he'd gone to get the rental car—but he was surprised she was tugging Whitney behind her. Christie was furious, too, judging by the way she glared at him, her jaw clenched and her eyes blazing. She stood just over the threshold, oblivious that Buster danced around her, wanting attention.

"*Tell* her," she ordered him.

Jack swallowed against the cotton balls in his throat.

"So help me God, Jack, if you don't tell her, I *will*. You can't keep people in the dark."

"I know." His voice sounded hoarse, weak, and as indefensible as he felt. An idiot, that's what he was— a fucking freak. He had honestly allowed himself to believe he was making headway, but he wasn't, not really. He was still the same guy he'd been since the day the bomber blew those kids sky-high.

"She means something to you," Christie said, looking near to tears. "Is this what you want to do?"

"Do I?" Whitney's gaze was on Jack, her brows knit in a frown of frustration and seriousness and *hurt*.

Damn it all to hell, Jack had hurt her.

"*Tell* her," Christie said.

"Tell me *what?*" Whitney demanded.

Jack tried. God, he tried, but the cotton balls were in his mouth, and his tongue felt thick.

"Okay." Christie nodded as if she were gearing up to step into a prizefight. She kept her gaze steady on Jack. "Just so you know, Whitney, my brother called me from the airport this morning in the midst of a full-on panic attack."

Whitney stared at Christie. "*What?*"

"Yep, it's true," Christie said. "Jack gets them all the time because he has Post Traumatic—"

"Okay." Jack threw up a hand. He swallowed hard again. He was mortified to see he was trembling. Rivulets of sweat slid down his back.

"Okay what? Okay, you're going to tell her?" Christie pressed him, because God knew if there was one person in this world that would push back at him with force, it was his sister. "Then for God's sake, tell her already!" She suddenly let go of Whitney's wrist and walked past Jack, into his living room, and collapsed onto the couch as if she'd just climbed eighteen flights of stairs.

Whitney stared at him, her eyes widened with bewilderment and hurt.

He'd done that. He'd made her doubt herself, and him, and the two of them. She must believe the worst about him. He could only blame himself, and the worst of it was that it felt too late now, because she had seen him at his most vulnerable. No woman wanted a man like him. If she left him, she left him— he couldn't change it now.

"Is that true?" Whitney asked. "You have PTSD?"

He hated that acronym more than anything in the world. Jack clenched his jaw and gave her a single nod.

She dropped her bag and the pie tin, which clattered on the tiled floor of the entry. "Why didn't you tell me?"

Her question wasn't accusatory. It was...confused. It was the question one asked when they realized someone they cared about didn't trust them enough to confide in them.

"I don't...it's not very pretty, Whitney. It's pretty damn emasculating, if you want to know the truth."

"Don't be an ass, Jack," Christie said from her perch on the couch. "Lots of people suffer from it. It doesn't make you any less of a person, or any less of a man, for God's sake." She sat up and turned around and looked at Whitney. "For what it's worth, it took me more than a year of my brother disappearing from my life before I was finally able to get him to admit what was happening and get help."

"How...?" Whitney looked puzzled, as if she

didn't know what, exactly, she wanted to know.

"I served two tours in Afghanistan," he reminded her.

"Yes."

"Well, I…" He paused to swallow again. "I didn't tell you that I…witnessed some stuff that was pretty bad." He closed his eyes against the painful images for a moment. "And I was wounded."

"Right," she said. "Your leg."

"Right." But that wasn't the injury he was referring to. "When I came back to the States, I started having these dreams." He gestured at his head. "Sort of reliving the whole thing again. And then I would, um, panic. When I was in a similar sort of place, I would get the idea in my head that the same thing would happen, and I…I flipped out."

"What he means," Christie said, her voice kinder now, "is that he was in a market when a couple of suicide bombers blew themselves up and a lot of people around him and nearly blew his leg off." She winced. "Sorry, Jack. I know it's hard for you to say."

He was actually grateful that she'd said it for him.

"But the panic?" Whitney asked. "Even now? Here, in the States?"

"Sort of," he said. "It started with dreams, then panic, then attacks, I guess. Full-on attacks where I thought I was dying. I started having them pretty regularly." He tried to gauge her reaction, to know whether he disgusted her on some level.

"And now he has full-blown agoraphobia," Christie added.

Whitney's eyes widened. She gaped at Jack. "Of *course*," she said softly. "That makes so much sense."

Jack groaned under his breath and slid down the

wall to his haunches.

"But how does it work?" Whitney asked.

He was unsure what she was asking. "I don't know. I mean, the attacks are a physical response to fear. For me, it started with being uncomfortable in crowds. Unfortunately, it's turned into more than that, which now you've seen." The heat of shame crept up his neck. "My fight-or-flight wiring is all screwed up. If I'm not in control of a situation, my body has a different mind than the one up here."

Just saying these things out loud made him feel anxious. He felt so screwed up, so beyond repair. "I'm better if I just avoid people," he said morosely.

"But…but you came out of your apartment to the café that afternoon."

"You went *out?*" Christie said with great surprise.

"I made myself, Whitney," Jack said solemnly. "I wanted to be there for you."

Even that admission made him feel ashamed. How hard could it possibly be to go see an empty café? Impossible for someone like him.

"Have you always been anxious?" she asked.

Jack shook his head.

"Not him," Christie piped in. "But our mother has severe anxieties. It runs in families, you know."

Whitney looked surprised by that. "Is there a cure?"

"He could take the meds his doctor has prescribed him," Christie said with a pert look at her brother.

Jack gave his sister a withering look. "You're not helping, Christie. I don't want to be dependent on pills—you know that."

"Because the alternative is so much better," she snapped back at him. "I mean seriously, look at Mom,

Jack. I have to go to Eagle's Ridge once a month to take her to get her hair done, to the library, to the doctor, because she can't get out. She is paralyzed outside her house."

"I'm not Mom." Jack shifted his gaze to Whitney. "It's not an inherited condition, Christie—"

"Except that if anyone in the family is prone to it, chances are that others—"

"It's not the same thing," he snapped. "My disorder is curable! Hers is just who she is. I've been working on it with a psychiatrist—"

"On Skype, because you can't make it to her office," Christie interjected.

"Okay." Whitney held her hands up. "Okay, okay."

Christie folded her arms defensively. "Well, it's true," she said. "And I know he won't tell her everything."

Whitney released a breath. "Is the psychiatrist helping?" she asked softly.

"Some," he admitted. "I'm learning how to assess things and find…" He could hardly say the words. "Find my safe space," he muttered. He, a former Marine. It was humiliating to utter those words aloud—a soldier was supposed to be the one protecting everyone else. Not looking for his safe space.

"He's supposed to go out and put himself in those difficult situations to practice his coping skills, but he doesn't," Christie said.

"I was going to do it today," he argued. "I tried."

"Wait," Whitney said. "You didn't go to the funeral?"

Jack was so ashamed he couldn't look her in the

eye. He shook his head. "I had to pick up a car at the airport. When I got there, it was really crowded, and someone blew their car horn, and…" He didn't finish his thought. He didn't need to—they both understood he'd lost his shit in the middle of the airport.

The shame was so deep it felt as though he were choking.

Whitney was suddenly at his side. She slid down the wall beside him and put her hand on the fist he had pressed against his knee.

"Oh Jack," Christie said sorrowfully. "You didn't take some of the anxiety meds with you?"

With a clenched jaw, he shook his head. "I can't think or function when I take them, and I didn't want to risk running into any of the guys, acting like a zombie. I can't… I can't live like that."

"But can you live like this?" Christie asked quietly.

Jack hated himself. He hated that he wasn't stronger, couldn't conquer something that seemed so ridiculous.

Christie sighed. "It doesn't help that the whole world will deliver whatever you need to your door. It's allowed you to close yourself off and make everything worse."

"Oh my God," Whitney said. "You're talking about me."

"She's not talking about you," Jack said.

"But she is—I get it. I come with food and cook it for you. Your laundry is done for you, the flowers are delivered—even your dog is walked by someone who comes to your door. You never have to leave your house," she said, her voice full of awe.

"America is a great country," Jack muttered. He

pushed himself up and walked to the windows overlooking the city. Christie was right—the privilege of living in this country had made it easy to disconnect from the real world and hide.

He heard Christie get up.

She walked to stand beside him and put her arm around his waist. "You need someone you can trust to help you. And you need to take your prescriptions until you get to a place where you can manage the fears."

"Is that all you have to do?" Whitney asked, appearing on his other side.

Is that all. What sort of man couldn't walk outside of his apartment without fear? "Supposedly, the anxiety that causes the panic will decrease if I find myself in a bad situation and get through it. If I can learn to talk myself down." He could hear Dr. Pratt explaining the whole concept of exposure therapy to him. *If you expose yourself to the anxiety and learn to manage the symptoms, your body will eventually learn there is nothing to fear.*

"Do you trust me?" Whitney asked.

He smiled sadly. "You're looking at the two people in all the world I trust."

"Then I'll help you," Whitney said.

"*No,*" Jack said immediately. He turned his back to the windows and stalked to the kitchen bar.

"Why not?" Whitney asked.

"Because, Whitney, I don't want to be a burden. I don't want to be the guy in a relationship who has to lean on his girl for help."

"Oh." Christie perked up. "Is this a relationship?"

"I don't know," Whitney said. "*Is* it, Jack?"

"Come on." He frowned at her. "You know it is."

"No, I don't know. I thought it was, but now...now I wonder if it's been more convenient than real. Maybe you would feel differently if you were out in the world with me, but in here, there's no other option, so..."

Jack's pulse began to race with a very real fear. "That's not true, Whitney," he said. "I really care about you. I know we haven't been out, but this," he gestured between the two of them, "is very real for me. I care about you very much."

She looked at her hand. Her brows were furrowed as if she were thinking things through. "If you really care about me, then you have to know that I can't live in your apartment forever. I can't run your errands. I can't live my life never knowing if you will show up or not."

"I know that," he said, hoping he didn't sound as desperate as he felt. "I get that completely, and I'm trying."

"We've never even been on a date," she said.

"But we will, Whitney. On my life, we will." He looked to Christie for help, but his sister was studiously avoiding his gaze.

"When?" Whitney asked.

He couldn't answer that. He wanted to answer her, to tell her here and now, but he had to be completely honest about it—it wasn't as easy for him as it must seem to her.

She stared at him, her expression one of confusion and disappointment.

Jack grabbed her hand and pulled her forward. "You have to know how much I want to be there for you, Whitney."

She nodded. "Will you let me help you?"

Jack stubbornly shook his head. "Isn't our situation already uneven? I don't want to knock it that much more off-kilter."

"We'll balance it."

"Whitney, you don't understand—"

"You're right, I don't!" she said loudly, and yanked her hand free of his. "I don't understand at all, but at least I'm *trying,* and at least I'm willing to try to help, Jack! I'm more than willing to do this if you are, because I care about you, too. We can start right now. We can start by going to a funeral."

He snorted. Waved his hand. Wished he could disappear. "It's too late for that. I blew it. I let Lainey and Noah down."

"No one ever said that you have to be with a bunch of other people to pay your final respects. There is a grave and you can still say your good-byes."

"An *excellent* idea, Whitney," Christie said. "I think you and I are gonna get along great. After the funeral, you can start training him to walk me down the aisle. I want you to be there when Chet and I get married."

"No!" Jack said loudly. "You don't *get* it. I don't want your fucking pity, Whitney!"

Christie gasped at his outburst.

But Whitney snorted. "You don't *have* my pity, Jack. You don't have anything but the fact that I really like you, although God knows why, and although I'm mad as hell you haven't told me this, I still want to help you. If you're not willing to at least try with me, then I guess maybe this was more about convenience. Which is it, Jack? Do you really want a relationship with me? Or are you taking full advantage of Dinner

Magic?"

"Jack, if you don't let her help you, you're going to lose her," Christie said. "Is that what you want?"

Two of the most important women of his life stared at him, silently daring him to refuse them in that way females had of boring laser holes through your skull with their eyes. Jack was a loser, but he was no fool. He threw his hands in the air. "Okay," he said. "Okay."

His disorder might kill him after all, but at least he'd go down striving for something he wanted. He wanted Whitney.

Sixteen

The kind of help Whitney offered Jack presented him with a new level of anxiety he had not yet experienced, and that was true, abject fear—she was a horrible driver.

He hadn't really noticed it the day they drove to Eagle's Ridge—maybe because he'd been so mortified about having to be driven like Miss Daisy to Lainey's gravesite. He'd sat in the back with Buster so he could feel the dog's firm, warm body against his. He'd thought a lot about Lainey, about the last time he'd seen her, about the last time he'd tried to be in Eagle's Ridge.

He'd thought a lot about his freak-out at the airport. He'd gotten there okay, maybe because it was early Sunday and he'd managed to get a seat on the light rail in the very back, where he could see everything, everyone getting on and off. But at the airport, it was chaos and disorder, and someone had blared their horn, and…

It was a miracle he made it back to his apartment without police or medical intervention. He still didn't know how he managed to get home, didn't want to think about what a madman he must have looked like.

In Eagle's Ridge, Whitney had driven to the cemetery, and it was easy to spot Lainey's grave—the mound of colorful flowers piled on top was a testament to the kind of person she was. There were so many that the scent was cloying.

Jack was particularly grateful to Whitney for insisting he come. He had needed that moment with Lainey.

Since then, Whitney had coaxed him to the bodega, and to the nearest grocery store. She insisted they walk in the evenings when it was dark and fewer people were on the street.

He felt as if he were getting better, as though his courage was slowly coming back to him. But it was slow progress—he'd not been able to take Buster to the park, although Rain took him four times a week without incident. There was something about that park that seemed particularly sinister to Jack. Too many places for people to hide.

He had not yet been able to take Whitney to a nice restaurant, which he desperately wanted to do. Neither had he been able to meet Whitney anywhere. If she wasn't with him when he left his apartment, he couldn't seem to make himself go past the glass doors of his building.

"When you think about going out alone, what is the thing that holds you back?" Dr. Pratt asked.

"Danger," Jack said.

"What sort of danger?"

He couldn't really express it. Danger was black and smoky. It was the feeling that crawled up the back of his neck and warned him that someone was waiting, was watching, was wanting to see him dead.

"Do you think it is a terrorist?" Dr. Pratt asked.

"Maybe."

"Waiting specifically for you?"

"No, of course not," he said, feeling foolish. But that's exactly what it felt like.

"And when your girlfriend is with you, you don't feel as if anyone is waiting?"

"I do," he admitted. "But it seems less likely somehow. It seems impossible to me that anyone would hurt Whitney."

Dr. Pratt nodded. "I would like to see you venture further afield with Whitney," she said as she made a note. "But I'd also like you to try to get out on your own. Ask yourself these questions before you go out." She held up a finger. "One, would a terrorist or anyone else be waiting specifically for me, today, on this path?"

Jack nodded.

"Two." Another finger popped up. "Does anyone else on the street seem panicked, or are there any signals that would indicate it's anything but a normal, typical day?"

"Okay," he said.

"And three, when you get to each street corner, I want you to tell yourself: I walked a block and nothing happened. I've walked two blocks and nothing happened. I've walked three blocks and nothing happened, and so forth."

Jack rubbed his nape and glanced at the window. He couldn't imagine walking more than two blocks, tops. Once his apartment building was out of sight, he was toast. "Okay," he said.

"Jack," Dr. Pratt said.

He turned back to his computer screen.

"Do you realize the progress you've made?"

"I guess," he said uncertainly.

"This week, you've been out three times, and it's been without medicine."

A small smile tugged at the corner of his lips. "Told you," he muttered.

She smiled. "We'll talk later this week?"

"Yeah," he said.

When he'd finished the call, he walked to his window and looked down at the people on the street. He didn't have the urge to believe they were coming for him anymore. Dr. Pratt was right—he was getting better.

But there was a new anxiety, and it was all Whitney's fault. Her driving was enough to make entire nations of drivers fear her.

Speaking of Whitney, he had to get ready to go, which meant he also had to do the three minutes of meditation Whitney insisted he do before going out. She'd read online that it was helpful for agoraphobia, and made it clear she would not accept any argument. Today was a big day—they were driving up to Christie's today and were going to spend the night in her new house. It was risky, and Jack had packed the pill bottles he never touched just in case. He hadn't had a full-scale attack in front of Whitney, and he was determined to not start now.

When Whitney texted to tell him she was downstairs, Jack hooked Buster's leash on him, picked up his bag, and took three deep, cleansing breaths as Buster tugged him toward the door. He calmly walked out his door and locked it, rode the elevator down with his dog, said hello to Frank and asked about his arthritis, and walked on to the glass doors.

This was where he always faltered. Through those doors, there were people everywhere, moving with purpose. It looked chaotic and disorderly, and as luck would have it, as he and Buster slid out of the door, someone blew a horn.

That damn *horn.*

His phone buzzed in his pocket. He pulled it out. *Cop made me circle the block.*

Jack swallowed down a lump of apprehension as Buster put his paw down on top of Jack's boot.

A red car pulled up to the curb. The driver door opened, and Whitney's head popped up over the hood of the car. She waved. "Come on before the cop comes back!"

Jack's legs felt like lead, but Buster was ready, and had trotted out to the end of his leash. Jack's slowness caused Buster to stop in the path of a woman in heels and a pencil skirt and forced her to hop to avoid tripping. She shot Jack a dark look.

"Sorry," Jack muttered. Before he could take another step, a van pulled up behind Whitney and laid on the horn. A shock of adrenaline ran through him, instantly ramping his heart into painful overdrive.

"You're in a loading zone!" the driver shouted out the window.

"I'm just picking someone up! Hold your horses!" Whitney shouted back, and darted around the back of the car to Jack. She slipped her arm into his and gave him a tug. With Buster pulling on the other side, Jack was pulled away from the relative safety of the building and marched alongside Whitney to the car.

"I'm not an invalid," he said brusquely.

"Don't be grumpy." She opened the passenger door. Buster hopped into the seat. "Buster! You have to ride in back!" she scolded him, and let go of Jack, took the leash, and pulled the dog down.

The guy in the van laid on his horn again, and Jack's heart lurched painfully in his chest. The edges of his vision were starting to swim—it seemed as if people and cars were coming out of the woodwork, crawling around him. It took every bit of strength he had to hold on to his wits and put himself in the car.

"I don't have all day!" the man shouted, gesturing with his hand out his window.

"You think we do?" Whitney shouted back. "People are so rude," she muttered under her breath before she headed back to the driver's seat and pulled into traffic with hardly a glance backward.

A new, tingly sensation rode up Jack's spine. He grabbed the handle above the passenger door window and gripped it as if it were the only thing keeping him from flying right out the roof. "For God's sake, slow down!" he shouted frantically.

"Don't yell at me." She changed lanes. "It makes me nervous."

"I'm not yelling."

Whitney shot him a look.

"Okay, maybe I did. But I don't want to die in a rental."

Whitney giggled.

Buster startled him by planting his two paws on the console between the car seats and stretching his long body from the back to the front. "You didn't put Buster in a harness!" he said with alarm.

"A harness?" Whitney looked over her left shoulder, changing lanes.

"You're supposed to put dogs in a harness. Like a seat belt."

"You didn't tell me that. He'll be fine! Won't you, Buster-boo?" She took one hand off the wheel to scratch beneath Buster's neck.

Jack braced his other hand against the dash. Whitney returned her hand to the steering wheel, giggling.

"It's not funny," Jack said through gritted teeth. "After two tours in Afghanistan, I'm going to die hurtling through downtown Seattle."

"It's *sort* of funny," she said. "We're not hurtling. We're moving at a speed of twenty-five miles an hour. And besides, I have to laugh, because if I don't, I'm going to cry that my boyfriend is such a nervous Nellie in the car."

He ignored that. "You missed the turn."

"I'm taking Fifth to 90."

"It's faster if you—"

She suddenly slapped her hand down onto his knee and squeezed. "I mapped it out. I know what I'm doing."

"Yeah, well, I've only driven it a hundred times," he muttered.

She suddenly changed lanes again, pulled over to the curb, and stopped. She gripped the wheel and stared at him. "Do you want to go to Christie's?"

"Yes," he said, confused by what was happening.

"Then cut it out. I'm not going to kill us."

She started the car again and pulled into traffic.

"Says you," he muttered. But he bit his tongue to keep from begging her to take him back.

There were too many lights on Fifth, too many people streaming in front of them. His muscles tensed, his body prepared to flee, or to abandon him altogether in an apoplectic fit. What did Dr. Pratt say? Block by block, has anything happened?

No.

They moved on through a green light, made it two blocks, and came to another red light. A cyclist slipped between cars, startling Jack when he rolled past his door. Jack was forcing himself to breathe when Whitney pushed Buster into the backseat and turned on the radio. Jesus, the *radio?* There was too much noise—too much, too much.

The light turned green and she shot out as if she were trying to get in front of all the other cars, then merged onto the highway.

He'd made it. Through what, six or seven blocks? And nothing had happened. *Nothing had happened.* He began to relax. Whitney was driving at a speed that, while not safe, was at least tolerable.

"It's not so bad, is it?" Whitney asked, as if reading his thoughts.

"No," he said. "Not fatal, anyway."

Whitney smiled. "You're funny, Jack. That's what I love about you, that you can still make jokes in light of what's going on in your head."

That was not a joke, but he thought it best if he kept that to himself.

Christie's neighborhood was pretty, with tidy houses and lawns and big, towering trees. It was idyllic, the sort of house he used to imagine when he thought of marrying and having a family. That dream had died along with his rational thought a long time ago.

Whitney pulled up in front of a red brick, ranch-style house, with window boxes full of flowers and a freshly trimmed lawn. "This is it!" she said.

Jack gazed at the house. It was very appealing. He was happy for Christie.

"I think Christie has a surprise for you," Whitney said.

"Wait, what?" Jack jerked his gaze to Whitney.

"You'll see," she said cheerily.

"No," he said, panicking. "No, no, Whitney. I don't know what you two have been cooking up, but you can't... This is hard enough—I know it doesn't make sense to you, it doesn't make sense to *me,* but—"

"But you don't think I see how you struggle?" Whitney interrupted. "We've been at this for three weeks now, and I see it, Jack. I *get* it." She took his hand in both of hers. "You're making progress, you're really *getting* somewhere, and I won't let you talk yourself out of it. I won't let you slide back."

"Why?" he asked. "Why do you care so much?"

"I don't know. I just do. I care a lot about you."

Jack shook his head. "I'm a burden, Whitney," he said, trying to keep the emotion from his voice. "I can't carry my weight—"

"Don't say that again, okay?" she said sternly. "I haven't asked you to do anything but try. I *like* you, Jack, in case you haven't figured that out. I *more* than like you. I have all the feels for you, and I know—I *know,*" she pressed a hand to her heart, "that you can beat this."

She looked so earnest, so sure. Jack felt a swell of

something so tender in him that it surprised him. This woman had somehow turned him into a big, fat, gooey marshmallow. He touched her face, ran his thumb across her bottom lip. "I don't deserve you."

"I know."

He leaned across the console and kissed her softly, with all the reverence he felt for her. The sort of feelings he had for Whitney Baldwin were almost foreign to him. They felt stiff and unused and too brittle to uncurl properly. But they were slowly and carefully uncurling.

She caught his wrist in her hand, swept her fingers over his ear as she kissed him back. And then she broke the kiss and pressed her forehead to his. "I don't know what it is about you, Jack Carter," she whispered. "I swear I don't. Maybe I'm the nutty one." She smiled at him and kissed him once more. "Let's go see your sister."

Christie and Chet were waiting for them on the porch with hugs and beers. Christie beamed with happiness. "I thought this would never happen," she said jubilantly. She delighted in the chocolate cake Whitney had baked that resembled her house—"When I looked it up on Google maps, I got the idea," Whitney explained. The cake even had a small dog that looked like Buster peering out the window.

After depositing the cake in the kitchen, Christie gave them a tour of her house. She and Whitney migrated to the kitchen to prepare appetizers, and Jack and Buster joined Chet in the backyard at a fire ring.

Jack liked Chet. He regretted that he hadn't been

able to get to know him better because of his affliction. Chet caught Jack up on wedding plans, a new position he'd taken at the engineering firm where he worked, and then they chatted about the chances of the Seahawks making it to the Super Bowl this year.

Jack felt relaxed sitting in that green yard with the blooming honeysuckle and shade of the maple trees. He felt happy. This was the life he'd been missing— time with family, with friends, talking sports. He'd been robbing himself of the moments that meant so much in a man's life.

He had no idea how much time had passed before Whitney appeared with a bowl of chips and guacamole in one hand, a glass of wine in the other.

"Does Christie need help?" Jack rose to his feet.

"I don't think so." Whitney smiled pertly at Chet. Chet smiled back.

"What?" Jack looked at the two of them.

"She's coming," Whitney said in a voice that was a little too sing-songy, even for her.

Jack didn't like it. He turned toward the house just as the slider opened. Christie stepped through, grinning as if she'd just won the lottery. Behind her was a man. Little antennae popped up in Jack's brain, warning him, but when the man stepped through the door, Jack knew instantly who he was: Zane. Insane Zane Tucker.

A grin spread across his face. "You've got to be kidding me."

Zane laughed and walked down the few steps and gave Jack a bro hug.

"What are you doing here?" Jack asked, ridiculously happy to see his old friend. "*How* are you here?"

Zane smiled and jerked a thumb over his shoulder. That was the first Jack had noticed the pretty, gray-eyed, golden-haired woman on the patio. She smiled shyly as she followed Zane down the steps. Zane put his arm around her shoulders and pulled her into his side. "This is Harper," he said proudly, and with good reason. Harper was a doll.

"Hi." Harper extended her hand. "I've heard a lot about you, Jack."

"Only good," Christie said breezily as she passed them with more appetizers.

"Very nice to meet you, Harper." Jack shook her hand. He glanced back at his sister. "How did you do this?" In spite of his happiness at seeing his old friend, his antennae were still prickling. The notion that this could be an intervention popped into his head.

"Don't look so suspicious." Christie laughed. "Harper is the librarian in Eagle's Ridge," she continued as she put down the platters of cheese, crackers, and fruit on a table. "I've been taking Mom there every month and met Harper and we became friends. That's how I found out about Zane. Believe me, I tried to talk Harper out of it, but she seems pretty set on him."

"Ah, come on, Christie, show a little love for your old crush," Zane teased her, gesturing for her to come in for a hug.

"Not on your life!" Christie laughed, and perched on the arm of Chet's chair. "He used to give me noogies," she explained to Whitney. "This guy," she pointed at Zane, "once jumped from Eagle's Nest Rock into the river because they dared him to. He could have broken his neck! That's one of the many reasons they call him Insane."

"But I didn't, which made you crush on me even more." Zane winked.

Whitney laughed. "What did they call Jack?"

"Romeo." Zane grinned at Jack. "He was quite the charmer—girls were always googly-eyed around him."

"*Was* and *were* being the operative words," Jack said. "Come on, let's sit."

Zane took a seat and propped his feet on the edge of the fire ring. "So how the hell are you, Jack? You've been kind of absent lately."

"Yeah." Jack hoped his expression didn't give him away. "I've been crazy busy."

"Dude, *no one* is that busy." Zane laughed.

"Right." Jack laughed too, aware that it sounded hollow. He had the urge to shove his fists into his pockets, but had to make due by pressing his hands hard into his thighs. "So what's going on with everyone?" he asked, desperately hoping Zane would take the bait and change the subject.

He did. "Man, where do I start?" Zane said. "You probably don't know that Ryder and Bailey are headed down the aisle."

Jack blinked. "Your sister Bailey? *Ryder*? No way!"

Zane laughed. "Apparently there was a way. Bailey is really happy. You know Adam and I have the watersports business, and that's going well. He met this woman, Jane, and they're pretty hot and heavy. Oh, and Wyatt's a bodyguard now."

"Wyatt?" Jack asked, imagining the Navy SEAL giving up the adrenaline rush to guard someone. "Doesn't sound like him."

"Agreed," Zane said. "But I think he's really

getting into it. Doesn't hurt that he started with a celebrity client who's pretty hot."

"Zane!" Harper said laughingly.

Zane grabbed Harper's hand and kissed it. "I have to call it as I see it, baby. Let's see, who else? Noah's back in Eagle's Ridge after, you know…Lainey," he said with a wave of his hand.

"Yeah." Jack glanced down.

"I thought for sure we'd see you at her funeral," Zane said. "You and Noah and Lainey were tight, man."

"We were," Jack agreed. His throat began to constrict. "I meant to be there, but something came up. What about Ford?"

"Ford, man…he's been trying to find himself since he got out of the Navy. I don't know where he's going to land, to be honest."

"I know what that's like," Jack muttered.

"You've been out what, two years now?" Zane said. "Last I heard you were still writing."

"Freelancing," he said. "I've had steady work writing for the military blogs and *Military Times*. Right now, I'm working on a big story about a clinic in Seattle that does contract work for the VA."

He and Zane chatted about that for a bit, but when the conversation lulled, Whitney asked, "So how long have you guys known each other?"

"We grew up together," Zane said. "But the seven of us, we really bonded in detention."

"Jack was a frequent flyer," Christie said.

"Not as often as Zane," Jack said.

Zane laughed. "You'd have to know Miss Woody to understand. I saw her recently," he said to Jack. "She's more gorgeous than she was, if you can believe it."

"I can't believe it," Jack said, and he and Zane laughed at the shared memory of lusting after the teacher. It felt good to laugh like that. It felt good to go back to a simpler time.

"I hate to be the one to break up this reunion," Harper touched Zane's shoulder, "but we really have to go."

"Go!" Jack exclaimed. "But you just got here! Come on, have another beer."

"Not this time," Zane said apologetically. "We have tickets to a concert I've been promising to take my girl to."

"And he's been promising for a while now." Harper smiled adoringly at Zane.

Zane reluctantly stood. So did Jack. "It's really good to see you, Romeo." Zane clapped Jack on the shoulder. "Great to meet you, Whitney. Chet and Christie, thanks for the invitation."

Jack didn't want his friend to go. He wanted to keep talking about Eagle's Ridge, about all the things he missed about his life. "Do me a favor and tell the guys I said hello, will you?"

"Better yet, come to Eagle's Ridge and tell them yourself," Zane said with a wink. "Hey, we've got plans tonight, but if you and Whitney want to meet us for drinks tomorrow, maybe we could work something out."

"We'd love to!" Whitney said before Jack could form a thought. Such as how he couldn't possibly meet Zane in a crowded bar in Seattle.

"Tell you what," Zane said. "I'll text you tomorrow afternoon and we'll see what we can figure out."

Jack smiled thinly, but Whitney said, "Great!"

They all walked out with Zane and Harper and saw them off. As they drove away, Jack lingered on the porch.

"Did you like your surprise?" Christie nudged him.

"I loved it," he said. "Thank you."

She smiled. "You know what's great? Today you're here and one day soon, you'll be in Eagle's Ridge."

He wished that were true. He wished he could go home tomorrow.

"Dinner's about ready," she said, and she and Chet stepped inside.

Whitney touched his hand before following them. "Are you coming?"

"In a minute," Jack said.

"Don't take too long. Christie made cheese enchiladas." She rose up on the tips of her toes and kissed the corner of his mouth. "It's going to be okay," she whispered.

Jack waited until he heard Whitney go inside, then swallowed down the cotton in his throat. He wanted to believe her, but his thoughts were suddenly crowded with the idea that after this very pleasant afternoon, after this return to a better time in his life, it would be soured by the fact that he couldn't meet Zane in a public place and pretend everything was normal. Just thinking about it made his pulse ramp up for full panic mode.

"Jack!" Christie called to him from somewhere in the house. "How long will you make us wait? We're starving!"

That was his problem—he was never there when

anyone needed him.

Jack swallowed again, and with his fists shoved deep in his pockets, he went back inside.

Seventeen

Christie had been beside herself with happiness when she actually saw Jack at her house. "He's going to be all right, don't you think?" she'd whispered excitedly to Whitney in her kitchen when Jack had gone outside with Chet. "I can't believe this is happening."

Whitney had thought it was significant progress, too, and had been all smiles along with Christie. *Look what we've done—we've beaten his agoraphobia!*

But in the week that followed, Whitney was less confident that his anxiety could ever be tamed.

It was true that Jack had made some great strides. But she had not fully realized what a foe she was up against until she learned he had not returned Zane's texts to meet up for a drink. He had completely ignored them.

"I don't understand," Whitney had said. "I'll be with you—you told me you feel safer when I'm with you."

"I do," he'd said earnestly. "You've changed my life, Whitney. But it doesn't go away in a day, and I can't shake the dread."

She'd stared at him, that familiar squeeze of sorrow against anger in her chest. She didn't want to be insensitive, but he was a big, strong man. Why couldn't he shake this off? It was just drinks. "You could have invited them here," she'd pointed out.

"Whitney, please," he'd begged her. "I just can't this time, okay? Please try to understand."

"I'm trying," she said. "I am really trying, Jack. But Jesus, you make it hard."

He sighed sadly. "I know, baby, I know." He folded her in a strong, comforting embrace, trying to soothe her.

That worked for a couple of days. Whitney could see that he was trying so hard for her. He and Buster accompanied her in an anxiety-ridden, yet successful jaunt to the little studio she rented, then watched her make cupcakes that looked like little flower baskets.

"You're amazing," he said, dipping his finger into the frosting.

He'd stopped complaining about going for walks and seemed relaxed when they added another block or two each night. Each time they ventured forth, it at least appeared easier for him.

There were moments Whitney was full of hope. But there were moments she felt as if his disorder were an insurmountable mountain that she was too tired to climb. He still wouldn't go into a crowded place, and he wouldn't go out alone.

After refusing to answer Zane's text, Jack promised to meet Whitney and her friend Louisa at a bar on his street. It was a quiet bar, without a crowd—she'd never seen more than a few people inside. She explained all this to Jack, and he had nodded along, as if he understood.

And yet, he stood her up.

"I don't know about this guy, Whit." Louisa sucked an olive off a little plastic pike. "Maybe it's me."

"It's not you," Whitney scoffed.

"Oh yeah? Then why is it he never shows up when I'm involved?"

"He's just really busy," Whitney said.

Louisa rolled her eyes.

In all honesty, that sounded pretty lame to Whitney, too. She couldn't imagine how Jack did it, how he offered that excuse constantly to friends and family and even to her. How exhausting that must be.

"So, did you decide about the café?" Louisa asked excitedly. "I got them down to twenty thousand a month, Whit. Someone should give me a medal."

Louisa and Whitney had looked at a half dozen properties since she'd seen the café. They both agreed, the café was the best option of all that Whitney had seen—the perfect size, the perfect location, with minimal renovation required to turn it into a coffee shop and patisserie. But it was still insanely expensive, and that place was going to require a bigger chunk of her inheritance than she'd planned. She didn't want to blow *all* of it on something that might not work.

You have to be willing to take a risk if you're going to do this thing, her sister Taylor had warned her when they'd texted earlier this week. *If you're risk averse, you have no business setting up a shop.*

It's not that I'm risk averse. I just don't know if it's smart.

Well, that's been the million-dollar question since you bailed on taking the bar, hasn't it? Taylor had texted without a hint of derision.

That's just what sisters did. They told each other the truth.

Which of my shoes are you wearing? Whitney had shot back.

The leopard print Manolos. Why?

Taylor's comments about the risks had bothered Whitney all week. *Was* she risk averse? How far out on that limb was she supposed to walk? Till the bough broke? She was supposed to be filled with sunny optimism, with that can-do attitude, and yet, she wasn't. She was worried.

"I'm still thinking about it," Whitney said to Louisa.

Louisa groaned. "You might lose it if you wait too long, you know."

"It's been sitting empty for six months, Louisa. I think I can take a couple of weeks to think about it."

"When *will* you make up your mind?" Louisa demanded as she dug her wallet out of her purse.

Whitney sighed. "I don't know. Soon, I promise." As her father was due to arrive next week, Whitney would love to have this thing wrapped up before he got here—it would give him less to opine about. But there was just something in the cosmos that was keeping her from pulling the trigger.

"Fine." Louisa tossed a few bills onto the table. "I've got to go. I'm having dinner with an old flame."

"Ooh la la." Whitney winked. "Have fun."

She stayed behind to close the bill out. As she

waited for change, her phone rang. She ignored it. She didn't have to look to know that it was Jack.

She gathered the change and walked outside. She paused there and looked down the street toward the high-rise where Jack lived. She wasn't angry. She was mostly disappointed. She thought of his coffee-brown eyes, of the way he looked at her when they made love, as if he couldn't believe she was there with him. She thought of the way he smiled, the light that shone in his eyes, and the reverent way he touched her. In some ways, he was perfect, the kind of man she'd dreamed of dating after failed runs with men who were better off with her father than her. He was sensitive and caring. He was tender and respectful. He was all the things a great boyfriend, a potential husband, should be. Except for his anxiety.

Unfortunately, the grip of his disorder was beginning to affect her feelings for him. She wanted to be supportive, but it was much harder than she'd imagined. It also seemed as if Jack didn't try as hard to understand how his disorder affected her. That, in and of itself, was a red flag. He'd apologized numerous times, had told her he was sorry for being such a burden to her. But he never really thought about how his disorder *affected* her.

A wave rushed through her. What was that—anger? *Anger.* Because she really needed for him to understand how it affected her.

Whitney struck out for his apartment.

Jack and Buster were waiting for her at the door of his apartment. His fists were shoved into his pockets, which Whitney had come to recognize as a sign his anxiety was ratcheting. He looked sheepish. Contrite. Worried.

She walked past him into the apartment. "You could have done it," she announced. "Did you even try?"

"I thought I could, too," he agreed somberly. "And I did try, for what it's worth."

She sighed irritably.

"I don't like letting you down, Whitney. I hate it. I never want to be the kind of guy who lets you down. I *want* to be the man you deserve."

Whitney groaned with frustration and dropped her bag at her feet. "I don't know if I can deal with this."

"Don't say that," he said.

"But it's true." She leaned backward slightly with the weight of his anxiety. "I don't know if I'll ever be able to count on you."

"Whitney, Whitney." He withdrew a fist from his pocket, put his hand on her arm, and pulled her forward. "Baby…have patience."

"I *have* been patient—"

"I know, God, I know." He laced his fingers in hers. "But it's a progression. It doesn't happen overnight. Dr. Pratt said it could take weeks. I need you to hang in there, baby. You were right—I've been making progress. And I know I need to make more. I *will* make more."

"Dr. Pratt also says you should take what she's prescribed you, too, you know."

He clenched his jaw. She knew his reluctance— he was afraid of them, afraid of what they would do to him, afraid of becoming dependent, of being unable to function without them.

She could read all those fears in his face and hung her head. "I want to hang in there, I do, but sometimes, it feels overwhelming. It feels like I have to carry the weight of your anxiety into the world and try to explain it, and honestly? It's embarrassing."

Jack surprised her with a soft laugh. "You're telling me?" He pulled her into his embrace. "Just hang in there with me, Whitney. I promise, one day soon, you won't have to carry the weight of anything but your own happiness into the world."

That was the way it always went—she felt his arms encircle her, and she couldn't imagine being anywhere else, and she gave in. She sagged into him. "What am I going to do with you?"

"I don't know," he said sincerely. "All I can tell you is that I am doing my level best, I swear it on my life. If it weren't for you, I don't know where I would be. Do you realize how much I appreciate what you've done for me?" He kissed her cheek. Then the bridge of her nose.

"How much?" she asked weakly, and closed her eyes.

He kissed her forehead, her other cheek, her mouth. "More than I can say." He picked her up. And Whitney let him, because she was weak when it came to him. In some ways, she needed him as much as he needed her.

He meant what he'd said—he showed Whitney just how much he meant it. He took his time, moving her through a tsunami of emotions and desire and lust, and of affection and love. That's what was beating in her heart as he lifted her to the heights of pleasure—love. It wasn't just pleasure swimming through her veins. It was true, deep emotion for this scarred man.

When they had exhausted themselves, they lay in bed together. Whitney told him that Louisa was pressuring her to lease the café and her misgivings about it.

"But nothing else compares," Jack said, stating it as if it was a fact to be added to the mix.

"Nothing else compares," she agreed. "Still, it's too expensive. I don't know, maybe this was a pipe dream to begin with. Maybe my family was right."

"I wouldn't go that far." Jack brushed the end of a tress of her hair over her bare shoulder. "Maybe Seattle isn't the right city for it. What about the suburbs? Or Portland?"

"Portland?" She came up on an elbow and stared down at him. "Are you trying to get rid of me?"

"Never." He pulled her down and kissed her. "I'm just trying to help."

"Sending me to another city is not helping. Not yet, anyway." She kissed his chest. "What about you? What's going on with your article?"

"It's interesting. Sharon's schedule revealed some things. I've been making my way through the appointments, calling people on the list, trying to get a handle on what went on there. My gut instinct is that there is a big, important story here, but I'm still putting the pieces together. I owe it to Peter." He stared off, his thoughts somewhere out there in the middle distance.

Whitney traced a line down his chest. "I never asked, but...have you ever...I mean did the thought ever..." She couldn't ask.

"Have I ever wanted to kill myself?" he asked for her. "No. My problem is entirely different. I want to figure out how to get back to the life I had before the Marines. Not how to end it."

Whitney propped her chin on his chest. "You want to be Romeo again?"

Jack grinned. He suddenly caught her and rolled them so that she was on her back beneath him. "You got a problem with that, Katie Cupcake?" he asked, and kissed her through her giggles.

The next morning, Jack made Whitney breakfast as she bathed and dressed to go out. "Pancakes!" she said with delight when she emerged from his room.

"They won't be as good as yours." He slapped three on a plate and slid them across the bar to her. "But they're edible." He winked.

She picked up her fork. Her phone pinged and she looked at the screen. "Oh." She frowned a little.

"What is it?" he asked, and proceeded to heap maple syrup on his pancakes.

"It's my dad. He's in town next week and wants to take me to dinner." She picked up her phone and typed back. *Would love to. Bringing a friend.*

The dots popped up, indicating her father was typing back. A moment later, his text appeared. *What sort of friend?*

An important one, she texted back.

Boyfriend?

Something like that.

Good. I'd like to meet him. I'll have Lois make a reservation.

"What going on?" Jack asked. "Your pancakes are getting cold."

"Just a second," she muttered, and typed, *Actually, I'd like to pick the restaurant if you don't mind. Can I text you a time and place?*

I'd prefer a call from my daughter, but yes, you may text me. I'll see you next Friday. Love you.

Love you.

She put down the phone and looked at Jack. "My dad is coming to town next week and wants to have dinner Friday. I'm thinking about the Italian place around the corner."

Jack nodded. "Good place. Eat your pancakes."

Whitney did not pick up her fork. "I told him I'm bringing a friend."

Jack's body instantly stiffened. "I don't know about that." He tried to smile. "It's a restaurant—"

"But a quiet one. I will make sure we get a table in the back, so you can have your back to the wall," she said, but Jack was shaking his head. "Jack, please. This is really important to me. I need my dad to understand that I am actually making a life here."

He put down his fork and braced his hands against the bar. "You *are* making a life here. You don't need me to prove that."

"Yes, I do. I need you. All my life, I've done what he's wanted. If I give in now, if I let him talk me out of this, he will run my life."

Jack shrugged. He picked up his fork. "Then don't give in."

"I can't help it."

"Whitney—"

"Don't Whitney me!" she snapped. "*You*, of all people, should know that sometimes we can't help that we do the exact opposite of what we want, right, Jack? I don't know how he does it, but my dad has a way of making me do things I don't want to do, and for once, just *once*, I want to be in control, and I could really use your support. This is what I was trying to tell you yesterday. I don't know if I can count on you." She stood up, intending to leave.

"You're right," Jack said.

She paused. She eyed him skeptically. "You'll come?"

"Yes," he said firmly, and straightened up. "For you, I will come. You can count on me."

"Do you promise?" she pressed him.

"I promise."

Whitney suddenly grinned. She sat down, picked up her fork, took a bite of the pancake and said through a full mouth, "Great. Let's go walk Buster."

"*Now?*"

"Now." She took another hurried bite, and another. "I want you to practice being on the street, because you'll have to meet me there. And we can walk by the restaurant and choose which table."

"God, you and Pratt." He pointed at her with his fork. "But I gotta say, I like how you're thinking like an agoraphobe."

She smiled. "I'm learning." As hard as it was, Whitney was once again determined to understand and to help. She would just slather the small stain of doubt that it was possible to help someone like Jack on the rest of her pancake and eat it.

Eighteen

———◆———

Whitney was so determined to drag Jack back into the land of the living that he was inspired to be dragged. Whitney was right—she needed to be able to count on him. And although Jack could see his progress, he needed to make more for her. So he made the decision to start taking the medicine. Dr. Pratt had told him that it would take two weeks before he noticed the effects, but after a week, Jack believed he was already seeing the benefits. After a few days, he didn't feel so drugged when he took them. He felt…normal.

He was feeling good about everything, really, except the article he was working on. The schedule Sharon had copied was blurry in some places, and in others, the handwriting illegible. There were enough names and phone numbers for him to cull through. But he was hitting walls at every turn. When he called the vets, he'd get no answer, or if he did, and said he was writing an article, many of them hung up. He was cussed out once, accused of being part of a conspiracy twice. But two vets confirmed what he knew—their appointments took weeks, if not months to get, and the follow-ups were just as slow.

But Jack needed more. He needed to know where the money for the appointments on the "official" computer schedules was going.

He was mulling all this over one evening as Whitney baked another cake. A lot of her baking accoutrement had migrated to his apartment. Jack had learned that when Whitney was nervous—which she was, as her father was due to arrive in two days—she baked. That meant his apartment no longer smelled like dogs and unwashed socks, but of pies and cakes. It was a sweet, homey smell, and he liked it.

He liked it so much it scared him a little.

He was at the kitchen bar, going down Sharon's schedule again when he ran across a name he had somehow missed before. "Diana Franklin," he said aloud. "Why does that sound so familiar?"

"Probably because that's one of the biggest event planners on the West Coast. You've seen the commercials, right? Diana Franklin knows how to party?" Whitney said absently.

Jack vaguely remembered that tag line. "Wrong Diana Franklin," he said. "I doubt she's booking an appointment at a VA clinic."

Whitney laughed. "I doubt she's booking anything anywhere. I don't think there is a real Diana Franklin. Here, taste this." She'd dipped her finger into a bowl of frosting and held it out across the bar.

Jack licked it off her finger. "Delicious," he said.

"Not too sweet?"

"Not too sweet."

"What about this?" She dipped her finger again, then leaned across the bar and dabbed another dollop onto his nose.

Before long, Jack had put down his pencil and had taken the bowl of frosting from Whitney and dabbed it into places that he'd never thought of putting frosting before.

The next day, Jack dialed the Diana Franklin number on the schedule. "Diana Franklin Events and Catering, how can I help you?" answered a friendly voice.

"Sorry, wrong number." Jack hung up. How odd—why would a party planning company be on the secret schedule? *Diana Franklin knows how to party.*

A party? For whom? He couldn't imagine the clinic using an event planner to host a party for the vets. Or for a staff party.

Jack called Sharon that evening.

"I told you not to call me again," she said.

"I'll be quick. Do you remember a patient by the name of Diana Franklin?" he asked.

There was a pause. "The caterer?"

"A vet."

"No," she said. "Look, I have to go. *Please* don't call me. I've already done enough." She hung up.

Apparently, Jack would have to get the answer directly from Diana Franklin.

Friday morning, Whitney called him. "Are you okay?"

"Me?" He quickly ran through the last twenty-four hours. No panic attacks, no close calls. "Yeah, I'm fine. Why?"

"I don't want you to be nervous about tonight."

Her dad, right. He'd been so caught up with the Diana Franklin business he hadn't thought much about it. He smiled into the phone. "I think the one who is nervous is you."

"You're not?" she asked skeptically.

Yeah, he was nervous. Not because of his anxiety—it was definitely there, definitely undulating in him. But because this was about Whitney. She mattered, and this was her *dad.* There was an unspoken tension between fathers and their daughter's lovers, and Jack had faced it before. He knew the tension, knew the nerves, and it was so...*normal.* A normal anxiety.

"Well?" she pressed.

"A little," he admitted.

"Are you up for it?"

He'd walked to the restaurant several times. Not gone in, of course, and he preferred to go when few people were out. But he'd proved to himself that he could do it. And yesterday, he'd gone in the *middle of the day,* had walked around to the restaurant and back. His pulse had raced, but he had not broken into a sweat. He had not panicked. He truly believed he could do this. "I'm up for it, Whitney," he assured her.

"Remember, seven p.m. Please don't be late. Dad hates it when people are late."

"Is there anything he does like?" Jack asked laughingly.

"Golf. What are you wearing?"

He looked down. "Jeans. And my favorite Pearl Jam T-shirt."

"Not *now*, Jack," Whitney exclaimed. "For dinner! Listen, wear the blue shirt with the dark-blue suit."

"You've been in my closet?"

"A dozen times. And shave. I love the scruff, but—"

"But let me guess," he interrupted. "Dear old Dad doesn't like it when men don't shave."

"You guessed it."

This was beginning to sound like an evening with a drill sergeant.

"You would not believe some of the rules he had for us growing up. My brother wasn't allowed to play football because of the potential to break a wrist or hand, which would have impacted his ability to become a doctor. And Taylor had to take singing lessons because Dad was convinced she was pretty enough to be in a beauty pageant. I mean, look, I love my dad, I really do, but he gets an idea in his head and it's Katie-bar-the-door."

"Whitney?"

"What?"

"Take a breath. And listen to me. Remember that this is your dream, not his. *Your* dream doesn't have to be proceeding like he thinks it should. Because it's *your* dream. Don't let him take it from you, okay? He can only tear the dream down if you let him."

"Right." She sighed. "Jack? I really like you."

"I know."

"A *lot*," she added.

He couldn't guess where she was going with this. "The feeling is entirely mutual."

"I know, but…but I think it might be big. Like a really *big* like you, like you."

Jack glanced at the window, his thoughts swirling. He really liked her, too. More than liked her.

"Why aren't you saying anything?"

Because he felt the same way. Because he was crazy about her, and in the chaos of working through this anxiety, and his article, and her dad coming, he hadn't thought of how or when he would tell her. But he didn't want to do it on the phone. His feelings required a much bigger stage. He dragged his fingers through his hair, thinking.

"Oh God," she said. "I said something really stupid, didn't I? I walked right out on the relationship plank."

"The what?"

"I mean, do you…don't you think we have something kind of cool?" she asked.

"Yes, of course I do." He was trying to form the words to say it, to make his declaration. "I'm getting there. I'm—"

"You're right," she said. "I shouldn't have said anything—"

"I didn't say—"

"And anyway, I have enough to think about with seeing Dad tonight. Okay, I'll let you go, but remember, *don't be late.*"

"I remember," he said. "But Whitney, I was trying—"

She'd hung up before he could fix it.

It was just as well. He wanted to tell her in the right way how he felt about her. How much she'd done for him. How he loved her. How he truly, deeply, madly loved her.

He got a cup of coffee, glanced at the suit she'd scoped out in his closet—when was the last time he'd needed a suit?—and then picked up his phone and dialed the number on the secret schedule.

"Diana Franklin Events and Catering, how may I

help you?" a young woman said on the other end.

"May I speak to Diana Franklin please?" he asked.

"Diana Franklin is the name of our company—there is no one actually here by that name. Are you calling about an event?"

"Yes," he said. Sure, why not.

"I can put you through to our manager, Lindsey Richmond."

"That would be great," Jack said, and quickly sorted out what to say. A moment later, a woman answered.

"Hi," Jack said. "This is kind of a strange question, but are you familiar with Victory Health Services?"

"Yes!" she chirped. "We've planned some of their events."

Jack's mind leapt. *Events.* "I was at one of those events and was interested in doing something like that."

"Which event did you attend?" she asked. "The one at the Edgewater Hotel? Or the one at the Seattle Golf Club?"

Jack was stunned. Victory Health Services was hosting events at one of the priciest hotels in Seattle? And at the exclusive Seattle Golf Club?

"The Edgewater," he said.

"What would you like to know?"

"I'd like to have a look at the menu. And get a ballpark on costs," he said.

"Sure! I'll need some basic information, and then I'll have Steve Simmons give you a call—"

"Oh see, here's the thing," he said, thinking quickly. "We're having a board meeting tonight, and

I'm worried there will be a majority vote for another event planning agency. I really need to bring something to the table tonight."

She hesitated. "I'm sorry, but Mr. Simmons is the one who would have that information. Unfortunately, he is heading up an event at the Fairmont Olympic Hotel tonight and won't be able to speak to you. If I could just get some information from you first?"

"Maybe you could call him for me," Jack suggested. "Shouldn't take more than a minute or two."

But on the other end of the line, Lindsey Richmond was not having it. "Who did you say you were again?"

"I didn't, but my name is Jack Carter."

"With who, may I ask?"

Jack sighed. "*Military Times*. Here's the thing, Lindsey. I'm writing an article for—"

"We do not give out information about our clients," she said crisply.

"Even if your client is misusing government funds?"

"Mr. Carter, if you have a legitimate question, I suggest you call our headquarters and ask our legal team to help you." She hung up.

Shit. He threw his phone on the bed, linked his hands on top of his head and walked a tight circle. He couldn't lose this lead.

A thought occurred to him—Fairmont Olympic was not very far from here. Granted, it was farther than he'd been in a very long while, but not *that* far. He could get to the hotel, corner this Steve guy and get what he was after before anyone warned him off when he waltzed into work tomorrow.

There was the issue of the hotel, and a crowd of people, but Jack told himself it would be good practice for tonight, and he was taking his pills. His muscles and heart tensed, arguing with his brain. *Too far, too much,* they said. But Jack had to try. He had to appeal to Steve Simmons's sense of right and wrong. He had to do it for Peter.

He glanced at his watch. It was four o'clock. He had three hours. He could get up there, talk to Simmons, then be back in time for dinner. He tried to ignore the uptick in his pulse, the niggling signs of panic.

Jack turned and looked at the three amber pill bottles on his dresser. "I have to do this and I *can* do this," he muttered. "You proved it to me, Whitney. I can do this."

He picked up one of the pill bottles and opened it.

Nineteen

———◆———

At five to seven, Jack was nowhere to be seen. Whitney paced outside the restaurant, her thumbs flying over her phone. *Where are you?!?*

"Whitney?"

She'd hardly glanced at the black sedan pulling up to the curb until her father stepped out and said her name. He looked as distinguished as ever, with his silver hair neatly combed, his impeccably tailored suit, his clean-shaven face. He smiled and held out his arms. "You're a sight for sore eyes, honey."

"Hi, Dad." She walked into his arms, grateful for his familiar hug.

"Where's your guy?" her father asked.

"Umm…" She glanced at her phone. "Not here yet."

"Then let's get a drink and catch up while we wait."

That was exactly what she wanted to avoid.

At a quarter past seven, Whitney texted Jack again. *Are you coming?*

A moment later, her phone pinged. *I am running late. Please don't be mad—I can explain when I see you.*

But Whitney didn't need him to explain. She already knew, and her heart deflated. She had really needed him to be here for her. He had *promised* her; he had said she could count on him. His anxiety was unbearable—she wanted to be compassionate about it, but this? This was a deal-breaker. She couldn't abide broken promise after broken promise.

She looked up from her phone and tried to smile in a way that would hide her abject disappointment. "I'm not sure he's going to make it."

Her father's gaze flicked to her phone, but then he gave her a sympathetic smile. "Let's get our table."

Whitney turned off her phone. Jack knew where she was, and if he wanted to be here, he would be here. She was not going to spend the evening checking her messages to see whether he was coming. She had enough to handle with her father.

She and her father ordered dinner and caught up on the family. Taylor was handling a case that could go all the way to the Supreme Court, her father proudly boasted. Cameron was considering a new residency in a trauma hospital in Los Angeles. Mom and her tennis partner had won a trophy at the club in a doubles tournament. It was pleasant, comfortable conversation.

Until her father put down his fork and smiled at her. "Enough about the other Baldwins," he said. "I want to hear about you and your project."

Here it was, the point in the evening she would be

forced to report on her failed, miserable little "project." But it wasn't a project, it was her life. And damn it, she was not going to be ashamed or cowed by him. She had given this chance everything she had. She drew a breath and confessed, "It's not going great."

Her father arched a dark brow. "No?"

"I have found several boutique cafes and coffee shops that would be happy to take my baking, but not without a health department certificate. I can't get a health department certificate until I have a suitable kitchen. I can't get a suitable kitchen because everything is either in the wrong location, too small or too big or too expensive."

"Ah," he said. "I was afraid of that."

Yes, she was well aware.

"But I find it hard to believe that in all of Seattle, you can't find a place to work for you."

"Actually, I found a great café that would be perfect," she said. "But it's too expensive. I mean, I could swing it, but it would take most of what I have to lease it and set up shop. So if it didn't work out, I would lose all my inheritance with nothing to show for it."

"I'm glad you recognized that. How much?" her father asked.

She winced.

"How much?" he asked again.

"Well…my realtor got it down to twenty," she said.

Her father stared at her, clearly surprised.

"A month," she added quietly.

He sank back in his chair and drew a long breath. "Whitney…you simply can't afford that."

"Dad, with all due respect, you don't know that," she said defensively.

"With all due respect, I think I do. I have administered your trust for a few years."

Damn it—family business was the worst for keeping anything close to the vest.

"I'm going to appeal to you, as an adult, not to sign anything that ties you into that amount of money per month," he said. "It would be disastrous."

His tone snapped something in her. He sounded as if he were talking to an idiot. "I didn't say I was going to do it!" she said angrily. "Why do you think I haven't done it already? Jesus, Dad, why can't you trust me? Why won't you support me in what I want to do with my life? I have a business plan. I have my inheritance. I know what I'm doing."

His eyes widened slightly. He put his hand on hers and said calmly, "I know, honey. But you lack experience. You've never started a business before, and you are not prepared for the sort of costs that can crop up. Unforeseen, unplanned costs. If you spend all that you have on rent, what will you do for contingencies? I need you to promise you won't sign anything until I've had a chance to look at it."

Myriad emotions bubbled in her. Old wounds, old assumptions. New, fresh wounds, a fear of failure, disappointment in everything about her life. Just once in her life, she wished her father would allow her to be her. She needed to figure this out and not have him figure it out for her. "I am a grown woman," she said low. "You don't have the right to talk to me like I'm an imbecile, okay?"

Her father sighed. He picked up his Old Fashioned and sipped. "You're right, I don't. But by the same token, you don't have to make a bad decision just to prove something to me."

There was some truth in that, she realized. Damn it, but he knew her too well. "I know why you're here," she said. "I know you want me to come home and join the firm and—"

"You couldn't be more wrong."

Whitney rolled her eyes. "Come on, Dad. You've been trying to get me to give this idea up for a long time."

"I concede that I was annoyed that I paid for an excellent education only so that you could discover you didn't want to be a lawyer. But Whitney, I have never wanted more for you than to be happy. If baking makes you happy, then so be it. I will support you. You didn't have to come all the way to Seattle."

She stared at her father in disbelief. "You've always said—"

"I know what I've said. Forgive me for not being convinced you really knew what you wanted. After all, you sprang the bakery out of the blue."

"It wasn't out of the blue. I'd been thinking about it a long time."

"I get it," he said. "You know what you want, and all I want is to help you. And the first way I'm going to help you is to tell you not to sign a lease for that amount. You will regret it."

He was confirming her private misgivings about that café. She suddenly put her head in her hands. "I don't know what to do."

Her father put his hand on her shoulder. "You're new at this. You will learn and you'll know what to do with some experience. But in the meantime, please, honey, allow me to help you."

Whitney thought of the life she'd been building here. Of the contacts she'd made. Of *Jack*. Jack, the man she'd fallen in love with, who was supposed to be here, who had promised not to let her down, but he had, and probably always would. The man who seemed startled when she tried to tell him how she felt about him, which had made Whitney realize that she was his crutch. He didn't feel about her the same as she felt about him because he needed her for different reasons than she needed him.

What sort of future did she have in Seattle, really? She had put so much stock into things that weren't really there. She lifted her head and looked at her dad. "Yes, Dad, please. Please help me."

Twenty

———◆———

Jack knew a doghouse when he saw it. It might as well have had a bright, neon sign welcoming him inside. He knew he'd screwed up, but he didn't know the magnitude of it. On a scale of one to ten, was this a ten or a twenty?

He did make it to the restaurant. But it was a quarter to nine, and Whitney and her father were gone.

He'd called a dozen times, had texted a dozen times more, but Whitney had not responded. He was desperate for her to know that this hadn't happened for the reasons she believed. He was desperate for her to know he'd had a chance to break open his story, and he'd taken it, and that the only reason he'd been able to take it at all was because of her. She had made it possible—Whitney Baldwin, with the many walks and encouragement, had infused him with the strength he needed to go out in the world. She had kicked open the door to his life for him.

The event, which Steve Simmons was running, was a charity fundraiser. Steve was not there when Jack arrived at a quarter to six with his pulse pounding so hard in his veins that his head hurt. Instead, the ballroom had been full of people, who assumed he had been hired to help and they'd asked him to check the mics. That request had sent Jack's panic into overdrive but somehow he'd managed to do it, in spite of all the warning signs of a full-on assault of panic building in his head and chest. But by some miracle, it hadn't come. He'd kept chanting *nothing is happening, nothing is happening* over and over in his head.

He knew the moment Steve Simmons arrived, because he was dressed in a formal tuxedo and swept in like a man who thought he had star power. He carried an iPad, the glow of which illuminated his smooth, botoxed face. He began to direct his small entourage.

He clearly believed Jack was part of the working crew, as had everyone else, and the two times Jack managed to get up the nerve to approach him, Steve Simmons responded with a crisp, "Not just now," and whirled off into a vortex of impressive activity.

At half past six, Jack still thought he could get to the restaurant just a few minutes late. He figured once the evening began, he could pull Steve aside, and then run—literally—back to the restaurant. Whitney would be upset with him, but he'd smooth things over with her. She'd be proud of him. It would prove to her that he was truly on the mend, and that was equally important to her.

At least that's what he told himself between his

internal chants of *nothing is happening*.

The guests had begun to arrive, dozens upon dozens, coming in twos and threes, quickly forming a crowd. Jack's heart raced painfully in his chest as more people filled the room. The edges of his vision blurred. He needed to be somewhere quiet and breathe, but that wasn't possible. This was too important—he was not leaving until he spoke to Steve Simmons.

He kept thinking about Peter. Kept reminding himself that if he let unnatural fear win, Peter's death meant nothing.

Breathe in, breathe out. This crowd won't hurt me.

It was a quarter to eight before Jack managed to get Steve Simmons to the side. By then, Whitney was not responding to his calls or texts.

"Do I know you?" Steve had asked curiously as Jack drew him to the back, where they could speak in hushed tones while a speaker addressed the room.

"I'm a journalist."

"Why are you talking to me? There are dozens of CEOs in this crowd."

"It's about Victory Health Services."

A strange look came over Steve's face. "What? Why? Look, I don't know what that's about, but I think you better leave," he'd said. "I have a job to do here." He moved as if to walk away, but Jack had put his hand on Steve's arm.

"Get your hand off me," Steve snapped.

Jack said quickly, "What would you say if I told you that Victory Health Services took government funds intended to help soldiers returning home with physical and psychological issues to pay for a fancy party instead? That's not going to look good for Diana Franklin."

"What are you *talking* about?" Steve had demanded, yanking his arm away.

Jack glanced at the crowd, then with his head, motioned to a door and a hallway that led to the restrooms.

Steve had reluctantly followed him outside, and with his arms folded tightly over his chest, he'd listened as Jack laid out his story. Appointments that never happened. Follow-ups that never went through. A dead vet, maybe more. Steve was appropriately appalled. But he hadn't believed Jack's theory. He'd pulled out his iPad and swiped across a few screens. "That can't be possible," he'd said, his gaze narrowing as he studied the screen. "They paid for the golf club with a check drawn from FSB Associates."

"Signed by whom?" Jack asked.

"Paul Calderini," Steve had said.

That was the name of the clinic director.

"I remember that event. It included the management of their San Francisco and Portland offices as well." He looked at Jack. "If what you say is true, a proper auditor would have noticed it."

Jack had given him a look. "We're talking about the VA," he said. "Do you have any idea how understaffed and overworked the Veteran's Administration is?"

Steve had frowned down at the screen.

"You have to give me those records," Jack said.

"I will not," Steve said pertly, and cradled the iPad against his chest. "This thing is my life. I am lost without it."

Jack ran a hand over his head. "My friend shot

himself because he couldn't get help from Victory Health Services," he said quietly. "While they were dancing the night away at a golf club, he stuck a gun under his chin and pulled the trigger."

Steve groaned. "You can't *have* it," he said, but he shoved the iPad at Jack. "However, you can take as many notes as you need for now. I will need that returned to me in an hour. And I never met you." He walked out of the hallway and back into the charity ball.

Jack had pulled out his phone, and had begun taking pictures of the iPad's screen, countless pictures of receipts and plans for wellness chats, high dollar meals, open bars, and a themed party.

In between, he kept trying to reach Whitney.

He should have called her before he left, told her what was going on. But he'd been convinced he would make it on time. He'd been walking a fine line between courage and cowardice, and he'd had to attack that small window of opportunity when he felt he could actually go to a hotel and confront a stranger.

When he had what he needed, he'd returned the iPad to Steve, then had run to the restaurant in dress shoes, his tie streaming behind him. He'd reached the restaurant in a sweat and was certain he looked like a deranged idiot. The maître'd' did not want him inside, but assured him the Baldwin party had completed their meal and left for the evening.

Whitney wouldn't answer his calls or texts all weekend.

This was certainly not the first time a woman had been mad at him, but it was certainly the worst. He had to wait it out. He confirmed his Dinner Magic meal kit was coming Monday, and he waited. He

purchased an expensive bottle of wine at the bodega—
going Sunday afternoon along with all the other
shoppers. He was ready to do whatever he had to do.
She would come in, and she would let him have it
with both barrels. He would beg her forgiveness and
take her out. If he could chase down Steve Simmons,
he could treat Whitney to a fancy dinner. And then
he'd beg and grovel if he had to. He understood how
much he'd let her down. He'd broken his promise.
He'd told her she could count on him. She could count
on him—in a weird way, the fact that he went to the
Fairmont and confronted Steve Simmons proved that
she could count on him. This treatment was working.

The challenge would be to get her to see that.

Monday afternoon, Tristan, the new doorman,
called up. "Dinner Magic," he said.

"Yep." Jack opened the front door. Buster sat in
the open door, his tail moving eagerly in anticipation.
Jack went back inside to straighten the candles, to
arrange the flowers—*which he had picked out when
he went to the flower shop, see how hard he was
trying*—but then Buster barked. Buster did not bark at
Whitney.

Jack turned around just as a dude walked in. "Oh,
hey, man, I'm Keith, your chef."

You're not a chef.

"I'm cooking your dinner tonight." He held up
the bag.

"Where's Whitney?" Jack asked.

"Who?"

"Whitney. She always comes," Jack said, feeling
defensive.

"Man, I don't know any Whitney. Wait. Is she the
one who had downtown? All I know is that she quit."

Jack's heart clawed its way to his throat. "She *quit?*"

"That's what I heard. Dude, could you call your dog? He's in the way."

Buster wasn't in the way; Buster lived here, and he liked to lie on the kitchen floor while Whitney cooked. Jack whistled for him. Buster came with his head hanging low.

"Just put it in the fridge," he said to Keith, and slunk down the hall, back to his desk.

She quit? Jack dragged both hands through his hair. His heart was beginning to hurt, but not with panic. With sheer misery. Whitney was being unreasonable. She was being totally, completely, maddeningly unreasonable.

Or was she? She'd tried so hard to accept him like he was, and he'd let her down in the worst way. Of course she was done.

The next morning, Jack called Dinner Magic and told the lady on the phone he wanted Whitney, not the dude.

"I'm sorry, sir, but she has resigned."

"Well, *why* did she resign? Did she resign because of me?" he demanded.

"What? I...I don't know," the woman said. "And even if I did, I would not be at liberty to say."

"You know what? Cancel my service," Jack said. "I don't want Dinner Magic if Whitney is not bringing it." He didn't need the reminder of Whitney or that he'd had to have a service like that because he was out of his mind. To be honest, he was sick to death of the sausage and zucchini and whatever else he'd been ordering all these weeks.

He was still stewing about it the next day and

cancelled Rain. "I'm going to take Buster today," he said, leaving a message on Rain's phone. If Mohammed wouldn't go to the mountain and all that... Jack was going to her apartment to beg her.

It was raining, and Jack didn't remember very well how to get to Whitney's. Thank God Buster seemed to know, turning left when Jack would have turned right. When they reached her apartment, Jack knocked. And knocked again. And then pounded on her door, yelling at her to please open. The rain was really coming down now, but he and Buster stood on her stoop, waiting for her to open the door.

Several minutes passed, and Jack climbed over a railing to peer in her window. He couldn't see anything, really. When a neighbor stepped out to tell him he was going to call the police, Jack told him to mind his own business. But he and Buster left.

For the next two days, he called her several times over, but it rolled to voice mail, until her voice mail was full and wouldn't take any more messages. Jack looked at Buster. "She ghosted me, man. She *ghosted* me."

He was a desperate man. He missed her so much that it hurt, a gnawing pit in his stomach. He missed her laugh, and how much she talked, and her cupcakes. He missed her ambition, and her sense of humor, and the way her eyes shone at him.

He loved Whitney Baldwin. He loved her so much, and even that, he'd screwed up. He hadn't told her on the phone because he wanted it to be special.

He called Christie. "Have you talked to Whitney?"

"No," she said, chomping on something. "Why?"

"I screwed up, Christie," he said, his voice

shaking, and told her what had happened.

"Oh my God, Jack! I'll try her."

Unfortunately, Christie couldn't raise Whitney, either.

As a last resort, Jack tracked down Louisa. She wasn't that hard to find—her ads were everywhere. When he got her on the phone, he told her his name.

"Who?" she asked.

"Whitney's boyfriend."

"*Oh*," she said. "You're using the term *boyfriend* pretty loosely, aren't you?"

"Probably," he admitted. "Have you talked to her?"

Louisa snorted. "Oh, I've talked to her—"

"Look, I screwed up," Jack said. "I want to apologize. Do you know where she is?"

Louisa hesitated.

"Please tell me, Louisa. Please."

"*No*," she said pertly. "You really hurt her, Jack."

"I know. God help me, I know. But she doesn't know why or how, and I need her to know that. You want her to know that, don't you?"

Louisa sighed. "Fine. She's in Orange County."

Jack was stunned. "She went *home*?" he asked in disbelief. She bailed? She threw in the towel? How could she have done that? She was only getting started!

"Yep. Went home with her dad."

Jack closed his eyes. All of Whitney's worst fears had come true, and it was his fault. He had failed her utterly and completely and he hated himself for it. "Do you know the address?"

"Why?" Louisa asked suspiciously.

"To send flowers."

Louisa snorted. "Well, that's not going to work. But if you insist." She gave him the address.

Jack thanked Louisa for her help, then hung up. He looked at Buster. "I hope you're okay hanging with Rain for a couple of days, pal. There's something I have to go do." He thought of the airport, of getting on a plane—God help him, he was breaking a sweat just thinking about it—and wondered how he would ever pull this off. It felt impossible.

But he had to try. Whitney was worth every panic attack.

Twenty-one

Whitney had no idea she had so much *stuff*. There were boxes everywhere, stacked in sets of three and four.

"What are you going to do with all of this?" Taylor asked as she maneuvered through the boxes.

"That's a good question," Whitney said.

Her mother appeared in the doorway of Whitney's room. "My goodness! We all have too many things, don't we? This makes me want to purge this house."

"Mom, this house is ten thousand square feet. You'd need a crew." Taylor plopped down on Whitney's bed. Below them, the doorbell rang.

"That will be the van, I suspect." Her mother went off to answer the door.

"Tell me the truth, Whit—is this what you really want?" Taylor asked.

Whitney tucked her hair behind her ears and

looked around at everything. "Yes. It really is."

"You're sure," Taylor said.

"I'm sure." Actually, it was the only thing she felt confident about.

It was hard to think about what she truly wanted because she missed Jack terribly. She was furious with him, and she wanted to kick his ass with the new stilettos she'd bought when she and Taylor did some retail therapy. She wanted to hate him, but she just kept missing him. She wondered how he was coping. She imagined him in the corner of his room in the throes of a panic attack now that she, his security blanket, was gone.

But that was just it. She didn't want to be his security blanket. She wanted to be his partner. She wanted him to be *her* partner, and Jack wasn't capable of that.

"It's time to do this, Taylor," Whitney said. "All my life, I've been swimming upstream—"

"Whitney!" her mother called from somewhere below. "Will you come here, please?"

Whitney looked at Taylor. "Do *not* go through my shoes. I have cataloged every pair."

Taylor rolled her eyes, but her gaze landed on the stack of boxes with Whitney's shoes.

Whitney ran down the curving staircase to the ground floor, nearly tripping on the last step when she saw just who stood in the door with one hand shoved in a pocket, and the other gripping a garish bouquet of flowers. The sight of Jack made her feel a little faint—her heart fluttered. She couldn't comprehend how he was standing here, in another city, another state. "How are you here? *Why* are you here?"

"Why do you think?" he asked. "Because I love

you."

Whitney gaped at him. Did he just say what she thought he said? He looked very nervous. But not in a suspicious way, as if he feared something. It was a different sort of nervous.

"Whitney?" her mother said.

"Oh. Mom…this is Jack Carter."

"*Oh,*" her mother said. She had, of course, heard everything about Jack Carter over a bottle of wine one night.

"Mrs. Baldwin, I'm sorry to barge in," Jack said. "I apologize, but I didn't know how else to reach Whitney. She wouldn't return my calls."

He was talking to a stranger. He was talking to a stranger in a strange house *as if* it was perfectly normal.

"We're in the middle of a move," her mother said crisply.

"I know. That's why I'm here," he said.

"Because of the move?" Whitney asked, confused now. Her traitorous heart was taking him in—*all* of him. He looked healthy. Sexy. There was something else, she realized—he wasn't perspiring. He looked calm and collected, and damn, it was so good to see him. But still, how had he gotten here? There's no way Jack would fly to California. Or drive. Too many highways.

"Yes, the move," he said to her. "I'm not going to let that happen. I'm just not."

Whitney and her mother exchanged a look. Her mother said, "He thinks—"

"Yeah," Whitney said.

Her mother moved forward and reached for the flowers he was holding in a vise grip. "Let me put these in water."

Jack reluctantly let go of them, then shoved his hand in his pocket and locked his eyes with Whitney as her mother stepped out of the foyer.

"How did you get here?" Whitney asked.

"I flew."

"By yourself?"

"By myself."

"*Wow*," she whispered, in awe. "I wouldn't have thought—"

"Me either," he said. "But, you know, some things are worth dying for."

He meant her, and Whitney's traitorous heart inched a little closer to Jack. "You shouldn't have come," she said, because the rational part of her was yelling at her to wake up, to remember what he'd done and not be fooled by romantic gestures.

"I had to. I couldn't let you leave Seattle without hearing from me."

"I don't want to hear from you," she said, and the rational part of her sat on her heart so that she could say her piece. "I'm really angry, Jack." She folded her arms across her body. "*Furious*. If you can come here, how come you couldn't make it to dinner, when I needed you?"

"Interesting about that." He took a small step forward. "I could have. But I—"

"You don't have to tell me," she said, cutting him off. "You had a panic attack. And that's the problem. I can't deal with it, I really can't. I've tried to be patient, but I need someone, too."

"I know," he said softly, and it sounded as if his voice might have cracked a little.

"No, you don't know," she said, surprised by how

much it still hurt. "If you knew, you would have lived up to your promise. You promised me that I could count on you. But I can't, and that hurts more than anything else."

"I do know, Whitney, and that's why I came. I didn't miss dinner because of a panic attack. I had a break in the clinic story and I went out to get it. I made myself go get that break, across town, and the only reason I could even think about going was because of you. Things got complicated and I couldn't get away when I said, and that's on me. But don't be mad at me for panicking."

She was so confused. The Jack she knew wouldn't go after a lead or a break or anything that required going out the door of his apartment building. She rubbed her forehead, and tried not to let her emotions weaken her.

"Whitney, you have given me life again, you know that, right? You have made me whole again. I can't bear the thought of not having you in my life."

"What does that even mean?" she asked him.

"It means," he stepped closer, his hands out of his pockets, "that I love you. That I would have crawled here if I'd had to. It means that I would suffer a thousand heart attacks to reach you. But I didn't. I'm stronger, Whitney. I'm getting stronger every day, and I won't give up until I am me again. And I won't let you give up on your dream. God knows I've let you down, but I swear on my life, I will never let you down again. I will be there for you. And because of you, now I know that I can be."

She was folding. Literally folding in two. She had longed to hear him say those words, all of them. "You love me," she said.

"More than I can say," he said roughly. He reached her and lifted her up to stand. "Please don't give up and move home. Come back to Seattle with me."

"I'm not coming back here," she said. "I'm moving all my things to Seattle, Jack. Dad helped me find a new place and put me in touch with a new realtor who has several places to show me. Not in the city, but in a suburb, where I can afford it."

Jack's expression filled with relief. He sighed heavenward, as if he'd just been released from the grip of something painful. "I thought I'd lost you." He suddenly took her in his arms, holding her tight. "God help me, I thought I'd lost you," he said again into her hair.

"You nearly did," she said. "But for some reason, I love you, too."

"Enough to marry me?" He kissed her neck.

"*What?*"

That squeal came from Taylor. "Did you just ask her to marry you?"

"He did!" Whitney said, stunned by it. Moved by it. So many wild thoughts and butterflies were suddenly swirling in her. She took his face in her hands and stared at him. She could see nothing but love swimming in his eyes. "Are you *crazy?*"

"A little," he readily admitted. "Will you marry me, Whitney? Do you love me enough?"

Whitney laughed, still stunned, but elated. "I *do*, Jack. I love you enough to marry you. Maybe not right away, because I'm still pretty pissed, and I kind of need to know if I can trust you. But yes, I love you enough to marry you."

"Is this for *real?*" Taylor exclaimed.

"That's my sister Taylor," Whitney said, and turned to her sister. "And if you don't take those shoes off right this minute, he's going to do it for me because he loves me."

"More than life," he said. "And I know better than most just how precious that is."

Twenty-two

J ack was beside himself on the day he and Christie went to Eagle's Ridge, picked up their mom, and drove to the bridal boutique. Christie was being fitted for her wedding dress, and he couldn't believe his baby sister could look so beautiful, or that she was getting married, or that he was getting married after her.

It was enough to make a grown man a little anxious.

He and Whitney were planning a big wedding in Orange County next summer. In the interest of speeding things along, they were planning it in her parents' backyard.

But today he was in Eagle's Ridge, and it felt great. He'd seen a couple of the guys. Ford was hosting a big party at New Year's, and he and Whitney would be there to announce their engagement. He'd been down to Adam and Zane's business, A To Z Watersports, with two beers and an apology, and as luck would have it, Ryder and Ford had come in. The four of them had spent an afternoon catching up and talking about old times.

The guys didn't press Jack on his absences. When they asked where he'd been, he said he'd been busy. It was easy to spin it—the article he'd written about Victory Health Services had been picked up by all the national news outlets, and had got the undivided attention of the Veteran's Administration. Who would have thought that a guy who couldn't leave his apartment would be freelancing for the *Los Angeles Times* and *The Atlantic*?

Whitney's dream was humming along, too. It turned out her dad was right about Louisa—a good friend, but a horrible realtor. Her new realtor had found a property in the suburbs that was perfect and affordable. *Whitney's Whimsical Treats* would open in the spring. Whitney had also leased a one-bedroom bungalow on a hill overlooking a small lake, and she and Jack and Buster spent many lazy Sundays there, wrapped up in each other on the couch, reading the paper, bingeing on Netflix and making love. Jack took public transportation to her apartment at least twice a week and had reached a point he hardly thought about it any more. Eventually, they would get a place, but for now, Jack was still exploring his new After Afghanistan world.

"I'm not going to lie, I still get pretty nervous in a crowd," he told Dr. Pratt. He was in her office, sprawled in a comfortable armchair.

"That's perfectly natural. A lot of people without anxiety disorders feel nervous in a crowd. The trick is to know how to manage."

"And I don't like flying." He shuddered.

"Then don't fly," she suggested.

"And I have this weird fear that if I drive a car onto a highway, I might not be able to exit."

Dr. Pratt smiled. "Now that's a little odd. I think you should work more on that one."

Jack laughed. "I guess so."

"You're doing so well, Jack," Dr. Pratt said. "I don't need to see you for a month. We'll monitor your progression, but I think in about six months, we can talk about weaning you off the medicine."

"No kidding?" Jack grinned. "Good. I really want to start a family."

Dr. Pratt laughed. "Talk about anxiety."

"What? Why?" he asked.

"Oh," she said, with a wave of her hand. "Children in general."

Jack left his appointment feeling a little nervous about the prospect of children. But when he told Whitney about it that night—at her favorite restaurant—she laughed and said, "Snap out of it! I'll be there, won't I?"

Yes. She would be there. And that was all in this world that Jack Carter needed.

THE END

About The Author

Julia London is the *New York Times, USA Today,* and *Publisher's Weekly* best-selling author of more than forty romantic fiction novels. She is the author of the critically acclaimed *Highland Grooms* historical series, including *Wild Wicked Scot, Sinful Scottish Laird* and *Hard-Hearted Highlander.* She is also the author of several contemporary romances, including the *Homecoming Ranch Series and the Suddenly series, including Suddenly Dating, Suddenly in Love, and Suddenly Engaged.*

Julia is the recipient of the RT Bookclub Award for Best Historical Romance and a six time finalist for the prestigious RITA award for excellence in romantic fiction.
She lives in Austin, Texas.

Visit Julia's Websiste
http://julialondon.com

Fnd Julia on Facebook
https://www.facebook.com/JuliaLondonAuth

Follow Julia on Twitter
https://twitter.com/juliaflondon

81591646R00136

Made in the USA
Columbia, SC
24 November 2017